To every one of you who think you might have a story to tell, I say, believe in yourself and go for it, I did. And to my husband, Chris, AKA Frederick, first reader, first responder and "BFF." And to Pamela Kelley for all things publishing. Life is good, writing is good, listening is even better.

"Oh what a tangled web we weave, when first we practice to deceive."
From Marmion, by Sir Walter Scott…

PROLOGUE

FIRE DAMAGES LOCAL CHURCH

For the third time in twelve months, a house of worship has been damaged by a fire of what is now considered to be of suspicious origin. Investigation by forensic teams shows a troubling and consistent pattern in the three fires. In each case, the fires have started on a Sunday afternoon, were the result of faulty wiring and initially were thought to be accidental. At present, there are too many questions and very few answers in an investigation of what could be the work of a serial arsonist who for some reason is targeting area churches.

Authorities have asked that anyone in, or in any way connected to, the affected churches who thinks he or she might have any information at all regarding these fires please contact ...

CHAPTER 1

J*une, 1867*

"Oh what a tangled web we weave, when first we practice to deceive."

 This quote from Scott's Marmion was the substance of the message in church this morning. The sermon was based on the eighth commandment, "Thou shalt not bear false witness against thy neighbor." Words to ponder, most especially now, when, I fear, in the personal confidence of these pages, that I have good reason for such concern. I fear that someone in my personal circle is bearing false witness against me, and for the moment, I am sadly perplexed and unsure as to what I might do in such an uncomfortable and unfamiliar circumstance.

 More Anon, LFW

OLYMPIA CLOSED THE ANTIQUE LEATHER DIARY WITH an impatient snap and retrieved the newspaper she'd dropped on the floor beside her so she could reread the article about the church fires. This most recent one was less than an hour away from where she lived—and might be working.

She knew that black churches in the south had been, and often still were, the target of hate-driven white extremists, but who in the world would be setting church fires in New England? Olympia Brown shook her head and refolded the newspaper. It just didn't make sense. Still, she'd been a minister long enough to know that churches and ministers can be ready targets when you have a grudge against the world—or God.

Olympia was unsettled. Totally out of sorts, neither fish nor fowl—well, mostly fowl—and Frederick, her devoted and occasionally eccentric English husband was keeping his distance. Eccentric maybe, but Frederick was no fool. She didn't often get into moods like this, and he knew it would pass once she had signed the contract for her next assignment. When his lady wife was between church assignments, she was a duck out of water, flapping around above the surface and getting nowhere fast. Olympia liked and needed the structure of a regular job. Despite the organic shape and nature of parish ministry, there was an all over rhythm and pattern to it that she loved and made her feel alive.

In recent weeks she'd applied for two positions and was now waiting to hear back. The one she really wanted —well, *thought* she really wanted—was a fill-in for a colleague who would be away on maternity leave. It would be three months in a mid-sized church of three hundred plus members in a nearby town. It had a competent support and administrative staff, a building that was in good repair and no latent landmines, at least none that were mentioned in the job description. This position would be like a summer vacation with pay. Easy and stress-free, and she could pull some of her old sermons out of the bucket. *Bonus!*

The other position was with a much smaller and older congregation in a nondenominational community church whose longtime pastor had been forced to resign after suffering a massive stroke. After years of relative stability and predictability, the members of the congregation were in a discombobulated free-fall and needed someone to help them through the chaos. Olympia did like a challenge and knew she was particularly good in crisis management, but at this age, did she want that *much* crisis management?

Small congregation, old church desperately in need of repair, falling numbers = falling budget = BIG PROBLEMS.

This church was farther away in a town that had once thrived during the manufacturing era but had been in a slow decline for some time. The low median income and aging demographics of the area stood in mute testi mony to the reduction in circumstances of its residents. While she had little firsthand knowledge of the congregation itself, she knew small churches always involved more feet-on-the-ground work for the minister than did larger, multi-staffed organizations. Add to that, small churches which have recently lost a beloved longtime pastor were especially fragile and in need of both grief counseling and anger management, in addition to regular sermons on a Sunday morning. This one would be a challenge, all right, and then some.

She'd learned in her cursory look at the review on the Chamber of Commerce website and from checking out the bare-bones church website that membership in the civil war era old South River Community Church had a way of ebbing and flowing the way churches do. Never outgrowing the number of pews but never really filling them either. Of late, the trend had been steadily down-ward, but they had faith this would change when things settled down

While advertising themselves as a nondenominational congregation that welcomed all comers, it was clear in anything she read that it was strongly Christian in theology and worship, scripture based by preference and tended to be politically and socially conservative.

That alone should have been enough to make her think twice about even applying for the position. Still, according to the pictures posted on the website, they, like every other protestant family church, drank lots of coffee, hosted pot-lucks and looked after their children and collected scarves and mittens for the poor at Christmas-time. Sadly, and also like so many other churches across the United States, they were deeply concerned over their decline and wanted desperately to turn things around.

The day before, in a telephone interview with the Fosselberg sisters, Thelma and Selma, both talking over each other on extensions, Olympia learned they were a tightly knit congregation with a strong community spirit —strong but currently devastated by the loss of Pastor David Edward Cameron and the tragic circumstances surrounding his departure.

"He had a stroke," they told her. "It happened right in the middle of his sermon. We all watched in horror," said Selma Fosselberg, who was quick to let Olympia know that she was the current church moderator. "I mean we were all sitting there. We always sit in the first row, don't we, Thelma? Well, at first he started slurring his words and then the whole left side of his face stopped working. He looked confused, then made a kind of gurgling sound and dropped like a rock onto the floor right there at the foot of the altar."

The Misses Fosselberg are thoroughly enjoying telling me this story, thought Olympia, keeping the irreverent thought to herself, and it clearly isn't the first time they've told it. As the conversation continued the two women explained that the church was looking for a minister who could step in quickly during the chaos following the tragic event, a minister who, if he or she were invited to stay on, would breathe new life into the congregational community.

Just not too much new life and for damn sure not too quickly. Olympia kept the instant retort to herself.

Instead she responded by saying she felt she was more than up to coming in for the short term and staying until they felt ready to make longer term decisions. She added that with the church in mourning and so much chaos and sadness around the sudden loss, a long term decision should never be made in haste just to fill the hole. A move like this needed to be made slowly, over time, with lots of input from members of the congregation. She did think it might be tactless to mention the fact that she was still waiting to hear from the other church before making up her mind, so she didn't.

Olympia ended the conversation by suggesting they all think about it for twenty-four hours before making a decision to take it to the next step, which would be for Olympia to come over to the church so they could all sit down together. Then, once they had the opportunity to get to know each other a little better, they could make a decision together, and then, whether it was yea or nay, they would all own it.

CHAPTER 2

Twenty-three hours later, Olympia was still undecided and still waiting to hear from the other church.

With the smaller church, would it be a case of Olympia to the rescue, a salvage mission where she would work her arms and legs off for a pretty paltry salary and with no predictable outcome? Ministry in a small church in turmoil would be a lot more mental and physical work than in the bigger more stable one. And while The Reverend Dr. Olympia Brown had never been afraid of hard work, the thought had occurred to her that maybe she was beginning to be ready to think about considering the possibility of slowing down just a little. Her short cropped, wash-and-wear styled hair was more salt than pepper now, and her waistline showed no signs of imminent retreat. If this was middle age, then she'd take it. Taking the easier path for her next assignment would not make her a bad person.

In making a case for the other church, she knew herself well enough to know that while she might like the short term position in a pretty town with a well-organized support staff and a good salary, she also liked a challenge—really liked a challenge.

The salary offered in the smaller church was proportional to the size of the congregation, small but reasonable, but her ministry wasn't about the money. It never had been, and in the end, the choice between the two churches may or may not be hers.

She looked over at her husband, book in hand and snoozing cat in lap.

"Frederick? I need some advice. Should I check my email for the third time this morning, or should I go make us a cup of coffee and divide up that massive cranberry orange muffin that's been calling to me ever since breakfast?"

"Mmmmph?"

Olympia repeated the question.

He smiled and held up an expository finger. "I have a smashing idea, my love. Why don't you check your email and I'll make the coffee and divide the muffin."

"As long as I get first pick." `

"But of course."

"That's a win-win, if I ever heard one. Thanks, love."

"Self-defense," mumbled Frederick disengaging the slender black cat and ambling toward the kitchen. Frederick didn't rush things.

Olympia ignored the spousal mutterings and was logging into her email when the clock on the mantel over the wood stove *binged*, and the incoming mail message on her cell phone sounded simultaneously.

"Double trouble." Frederick, pointed to the clock.

"We'll know in a minute, it looks like I have mail."

Olympia pulled out her phone and double-tapped on the email icon.

In minutes Frederick walked back into the sitting room carrying two mugs of steaming coffee. On top of each mug he'd precariously balanced a small plate with a precisely measured and sliced half of a cranberry muffin. Olympia winced, held her breath and thought about the tea trays they kept under the counter for such delicate purposes. On the best of days, her beloved was a total klutz with a propensity for overbalancing a load and underestimating the distance between two fixed points over which said load was to be transported. With a practiced flourish and not a spilled drop or a dropped crumb, Frederick set her mug and muffin down beside her. Olympia exhaled.

"What ho? Yea or nay?"

"One of each. One yea and one nay." She reached for the muffin.

"Come on, girl, don't keep a man in suspense. Which is which?"

"The bigger church said, 'No, thank you.' They told me they decided to give the position to a retired minister who had served them once before as an interim and who was familiar with the town and the congregation. A man who knew how they did things would make it so much easier for all concerned, so thank you, but no, thanks." She rolled her eyes.

"So it's the smaller one, by default. How's that sitting with you?"

Olympia hesitated and stared into her coffee for a long moment. "Well, it's not final yet. They've invited me in to meet the board. To be honest, I suppose the no from the big church feels like a rejection. Even though the reason the bigger church gave me is perfectly sound, I suppose I would have preferred to be the one to say no."

"And would you have?" He cocked his head to one side and looked at her.

She nodded. "I think so, but I'm not sure."

"So what's the problem?"

"Ego, probably, and I can do better than that, but I'm still feeling a little rejected."

"You're human."

"I prefer you didn't remind me."

"Eat your muffin, my love. It's delicious, and it's good for you—and if you don't, I will." He paused in mid-reach and looked over at the antique clock. "I wonder why she's chimed in on this conversation?"

"All will be revealed. And keep your grabby little English paws off my muffin!"

CHAPTER 3

On Tuesday of the following week, the governing board of the South River Community Church had invited a cautiously optimistic Reverend Olympia to an informal luncheon in the church parlor, "To meet a few of us so we can get to know you and tell you what we want for the church," said Selma Fosselberg when the invitation was issued.

The words, "tell you what we want for the church" should have been Olympia's first clue, and in some ways it was. If she agree to their offer, all of her professional instincts told her that this was going to be a tough little church. Now she was going to meet the power cluster. She knew that however they labeled themselves—the board, the governing body, the vestry—these were the people who ran the church, no questions asked, and by the sound of them, Selma and Thelma were charter members.

So it was that, carefully staged and orchestrated

between the crust-less sandwiches, the Jello salad and the cucumber enhanced ice water, she was given a walking tour along with an uninterrupted step-by-inch oral history of the white clapboard 1860s building and its surrounds. This included some civil war and abolitionist stories and the fact that another woman minister named Olympia Brown, what a coincidence, had been an early guest preacher in their church in the year 1868. In the very same pulpit you will hold, they told her. Her reward for all of this was Darjeeling tea in china cups with matching saucers and mounds of homemade cookies.

The running narrative and local gossip were provided by the same Fosselberg twins she'd spoken to over the phone just days before. Olympia would learn that they were the church's ruling spinster matriarchs. She knew the type, and it was a type. Beloved and revered, and not a little feared, by all until you crossed them. They would do anything for anyone anytime, until you crossed them. They donated hours and money and enormous casseroles and decadent baked wonders for every occasion … until you crossed them.

She didn't have to be told. She knew her part in this little liturgical drama. These ladies, with their full pigeon breasts and tightly controlled grey curls, who knew everybody's genealogy, family history and where all the bodies were buried, ruled the roost.

When the last of the cookies were gone, and the interview was over, they told Olympia that she had the job, and could she start that Sunday? Her answer stunned them. Yes, she would take the service on the upcoming Sunday, but no, she would not accept any kind of a contract until they listened to her preach and experienced how she handled herself both in the pulpit and later in the coffee hour.

"We all need to know each other more fully," she explained, "because in the end, it's not about sermons and how many names I can learn in a single morning. This is about fit. In other words, do the skills and qualifications that I bring to the position match what you believe you want and need in a minister for your church?"

She asked them to consider whether she would be a good fit for the congregation, and, likely something they'd never considered in the past, she needed time to decide if she would be a good fit for them. By the astonished looks on their collective faces, Olympia could tell that the very thought that someone wouldn't instantly leap at the opportunity left them nonplussed and gawping like fish out of water, which in some respects was exactly what they were.

"Then," she added with a genuine smile, "we can have another sit-down, and if it's a go for all of us, we can draft a letter of understanding and agreement."

"What's a letter of agreement?" asked Jeanne Lane, another member of the board, who'd proudly told Olympia she was a Mayflower descendent.

"It's like a contract, but it's specifically tailored to the needs and expectations of the congregation and the minister, the acceptance of those considerations and expectations including expected hours engaged in the duties of the ministry."

"Hours?" squeaked Thelma. "We've never talked

about hours with a minister. You just do the job. I mean, it's not like you are working at a bank or a grocery store."

"Or in an insurance company or a manufacturing company. You don't punch in or punch out," added Selma.

"Exactly right. The task of ministry is flexible. Some might even say it's a moving target," said Olympia. "Can we all think about a positive outcome would look like and then come back here to church on Sunday and talk it over? So, I suggest we all go home and think about what we want and need for this congregation."

"But … but," stammered, Selma, "what if you don't want to come? Whatever will we do then?" The stammer trailed off in a whine.

Olympia smiled gently. Her little attempt at moving-target humor had sailed right past them. "I cannot even remotely imagine a reason for that happening right now," she assured them, "but even if we all agree this is not the right place for me, I promise you I will stay until you find someone for whom it is right, and I will do it with a happy heart and an honest commitment. Remember, you might be the ones who decide that I am not the best fit for you."

"What will you do then?"

"I won't come back—or I'll stay on as a guest or temporary preacher until you have found the perfect pastor for you."

I can do this, she told herself driving back home later that day, but I still need to think about it, and what's even more important is that they think about what they are really looking for. It's a short, transitional assignment, and Thelma and Selma will no doubt be very useful in helping me learn how this particular church functions. I should have no reason to cross them … unless, of course, I have to. Olympia knew all about church matriarchs and sacred cows. Often the two were one and the same. She giggled at the image of two chubby cows in flowered hats holding teacups.

The following weekend, on a damp and humid Sunday in late June, Olympia was wearing her light-weight summer robe and as little as decently possible under it when she stepped into the musty pulpit of the South River Community Church. Once ensconced, and over and around the whirr of two ancient oscillating floor fans doing battle with one another over the pews, she looked out over the thirty or so curious people sitting in front of her, smiled and introduced herself.

She knew that her best bet on a first Sunday anywhere was speak about the value of religious and spir-itual community and then go on to tell them a little about herself and her own spiritual journey. If she could add to this some personal connections to the congregation or the town, she would score a perfect ten. Olympia was a professional—a very sincere and dedicated professional, at that. She had done this before, and God willing, she'd do it again. She looked out at their upturned expectant faces. I can love these folks, she thought. It's what I do.

Having made it through the first hymn and the story for children, both of them, she began to relax. She was about to extend the invitation for prayers of the people when she saw a woman wearing dark glasses, a colorful summer hat and leading a harnessed service dog, enter the back of the church. She stood for a moment and then took a seat at the outside edge of the last pew. Olympia never missed a beat, offered a quick nod of recognition to welcome her and continued with the established order of service.

When she opened her arms and invited people to come forward with their joys and sorrows and prayer requests, the woman in the back hesitated for a brief moment and then, with her dog at her heel, joined the small queue of people moving toward the front of the church. Olympia had no idea whether she was a member of the congregation, but from the sideways, curious looks of the people in the pews, Olympia surmised she was probably not. Other than the dog, the woman didn't seem out of the ordinary. She looked to be fifty-ish, a little younger than Olympia herself, dressed for a hot summer day in a flowery cotton skirt and top that picked up the colors of the hat. She approached the front of the church with an oversized canvas carry-bag slung over her shoulder and a tight grip on the dog's leash with her free hand. The dog, obviously well cared for, was a sandy colored shepherd-mix wearing a matching flowered bandana around its neck and a bright red 'service dog' vest and harness.

When it was the woman's turn to speak, she gave her name as Rayna Buxton. She told them she was really shy, and getting up in front of everyone was especially hard for her, but from the minute she'd opened the door she felt safe here and thanked everyone for that. She went on to say she was new in town, and she was looking for church home. She gestured to the animal standing at attention beside her and introduced Raggsy as her comfort dog. She reached down and patted his head and was rewarded with a vigorous tail wag.

"He makes life possible for me," she said softly. "I hope you'll welcome him too. Not everyone does." She paused. "But I do have to ask that you not pat him or feed him or touch me until I give him the signal. He's a working dog and very protective. Once he knows you, and you're okay, he'll remember you and be your friend for life." She smiled fondly at the animal. "He may be a dog, but he's got a memory like an elephant."

What happened after that was as predictable as a rainbow after a cloudburst. Lots of nods and reassuring smiles in Rayna's direction as she and the dog returned to her seat at the back. Later, at the social hour, the kindly people respected her request and approached her and the dog respectfully. They did everything they could to make them both welcome. Olympia, standing off to the side with her pale, tepid, revolting coffee and a cluster of cookies in a paper napkin, watched it all play out. She'd seen it all before, the churchly welcoming of strangers, and she knew that it was good.

This is what loving, close-knit, small congregations did. They knew the drill. They visited the sick, they clothed the naked, and they welcomed the stranger. On a bad day they held committee meetings, served tea and cookies and gossiped.

If Olympia was feeling the slightest flicker of discomfort in the presence and performance of the newcomer, she blamed her own newness and reasoned it away by reminding herself that she, too, was new that day, and we all handle being new differently. Don't we?

Olympia took another sip of the awful church coffee and winced. *What was it about church coffee?* Another holy mystery she would no doubt address one day in her clerically checkered career, but not now. Her husband Frederick would have called it gnat's piss. She smiled again and, for the time being, kept silent on the matter of the insect urine and bad coffee.

Before long the crowd began to thin, and the Fosselberg twins were zeroing in on this week's volunteers to help with the coffee hour clean-up. There was no escape. By way of a gesture of total welcome, one of the people they commandeered that day was Rayna and her dog.

"Everybody makes friends in the kitchen," they said, nodding agreement with themselves and herding her toward the kitchen.

The dog stiffened, pressed against Rayna's leg and made a low growl.

"Relax, Raggsy. It's safe. Good dog." Rayna reassured the animal before accepting the invitation and heading off with the two ladies. The dog, now oriented, was happily wagging his tail in the possible anticipation of a dropped biscuit or potato chip and virtually pranced along beside his mistress.

With that settled and Rayna and protector well in hand, Olympia turned away and went back to her office to familiarize herself with the space and to take some time to do a little post-Sunday-service wind-down and note making of her own. That, and there was an ancient but fully functional air conditioner grinding away in the single office window. She settled into the blissful cool and was soon lost in her work.

"Reverend Brown?"

She looked up to see Rayna and her dog standing in the doorway. She was mildly discomforted by the fact that she'd not heard them approach but instantly dismissed it as a startle reaction and waved them in.

"Well, look who's here. Come in, Rayna, and you too, Raggsy. Come in and sit down both of you."

Before the woman and her dog entered the room, Rayna whispered, "Relax, Raggsy, it's safe. Good dog."

Olympia pointed in the direction of the two visitor chairs in the room, a carved oak rocker and an upholstered wing chair. "Take your pick. I'll sit in the other one. I wish I had a treat for the dog."

Rayna held up her hand. "No, no, that's okay. I prefer that others don't feed him. He can get over excited."

"That's just being a dog. They all get excited," said Olympia. "Let me see if I have something in my purse. If I look hard enough I can probably find an old packet of oyster crackers or something."

Rayna shook her head more firmly this time, "Please don't. I'm the only one who feeds him."

This time, Olympia got the message and pulled back. "Of course. Sorry, it's just that I'm an animal lover, and food equals love where I come from. Now then, settle down and let's get to know each other. I do have to tell you, though, this is my first Sunday here, as well, and I'm not sure how much I can tell you about the church, but I'll do the best I can. And what I can't tell you right off, I'll make it my business to find out who I can ask."

The slender woman fidgeted with the end of the leash for a moment. "Um, well, I already said I was new, and that I was church shopping, but the truth is, I haven't been in a church since I was ten. I guess I didn't know what to expect after all that time. This church is so different than the one I grew up in. It's nice."

Olympia knew this was not the time to go into the details of nondenominational church theology. This was not about theology, this was about finding acceptance. There was a thin, anxious woman sitting in front of her who was clearly in some kind of need; and she had a big, beautiful, intelligent dog beside her whose watchful eyes told her, you can come this far and no farther.

"Tell me about the church where you grew up."Rayna flinched. "Let's just say the people there didn't always tell the truth." The look on her face indicted the subject was closed … for now.

Olympia made a mental note of the reaction and tried a different tack. "What kind of dog is Raggsy?"

"German Shepherd, Doberman and something else. Those curls in his coat come from the somewhere else. Maybe there's some Golden Retriever in there." She reached down and rubbed the dog's ear. "Like I told everybody in church this morning, I'm new in town. I live alone with my dog, and thanks to him I'm able to start going out on my own again."

The questions in Olympia's mind were multiplying exponentially. She made a silent note to self to write them all down when the woman left. She tried again.

"Do you live nearby? Walking distance? Driving distance?"

"I'm not allowed to drive. Not yet. Pretty soon, though."

Not exactly forthcoming, thought Olympia, who by now was giving serious thought to tearing her hair out with both hands but prudently and kindly did nothing. *Steady as she goes, Olympia. You've dealt with this kind before. You'll get there, or you won't. No, she'll get there, or she won't. It's not about you.*

The woman leaned forward and cleared her throat. "I used to have a red VW Jetta."

Olympia's ears perked up when she heard VW. Finally, some common ground. "I have a VW van. I've always driven VWs. This one's older than dirt, but I'll keep it going until I can't climb into it anymore, or the wheels fall off, whichever comes first."

Rayna responded with a genuine smile.

Breakthrough!

"Did you have a name for your car? I call mine Vanessa."

Rayna nodded. "She-devil," she added with another little giggle, "I called her that because it was bright red and I drove like hell. Oops, sorry for the hell, Reverend."

Olympia waved it away with quick shake of her head. They were talking, or more correctly, Rayna was talking, and the dog had finally flopped himself down on the floor beside her, more relaxed now but still watching everything.

Sensing a lowering of Rayna's defenses, Olympia

decided to stay with the fairly neutral car theme for the time being.

"So I'm assuming that you live within walking distance of the church. From what I hear, there's no public transportation here in South River."

The nervous woman smiled. She's quite attractive when she smiles, thought Olympia.

"Thank heaven for Uber and Lyft and cell phones. I can get where I want to when I want to, and like I said, I'll be driving again soon. This inconvenient hiatus is quite temporary. I'm just getting over my last round of chemotherapy." She pointed to her floppy hat and scarf. "My hair won't start growing in for a while yet, I'm afraid, but this works to hide the baldness and keep me from getting a sunburnt scalp."

"Oh my goodness." Olympia thought of her own daughter, who'd had a similar battle. "That's good news."

"I should be able to drive and go back to work soon." She sighed and smiled.

"It feels like forever. It really punched a hole in me in more ways than one, but it's all good now, isn't it, Raggsy?"

The woman is quite literate, thought Olympia, and rather than risking another circuitous meander, asked what she did for work.

"I'm a personal assistant. You know, a private girl Friday for people wealthy enough to pay somebody to do their shopping and handle their correspondence. Until I got sick I actually worked on the Cape for a member of the Kennedy family. When I can drive again, I'll probably look for something part time on the upper Cape."

She dropped her voice. "You probably don't know this, but there's a lot of hidden money there. They don't like to advertise their wealth, so they act and dress like the rest of us, but once you get inside the inner circle, well, let's just say it's very different from anything I'm used to."

Rayna was becoming more animated now, letting her guard down and speaking more freely. Raggsy, ever attuned to his lady's moods, put his head on his paws and heaved a great doggy sigh of contentment.

For a few more minutes they talked about the attributes of the town, the weather and shared animal stories. All neutral, all safe and all comfortably ordinary and everyday topics for casual conversation. Olympia was making mental notes as she always did when she had any kind of a conversation with a parishioner, or in this case a potential parishioner. It was a professional practice that had served her well. She wasn't sure about this woman yet, but for the time being, she willed herself to be a good and sympathetic listener. If she had any reservations, they would no doubt clarify themselves before long. The cancer story spoke volumes. The woman had been through hell. It likely explained why she was so thin and why she'd never taken off the flowered cotton hat.

After a few more snippets of chit-chat, none of it of any substance, Rayna began to fidget and then glanced down at the oversized watch on her wrist.

"My goodness, wherever has the day gone? I didn't mean to take up so much of your time. It's only that …" She paused. "No, never mind. We'll talk again I'm sure. And thank you. I'm definitely coming back next Sunday, but I have to get going now before the day gets completely away from me."

Olympia wondered what it was that she needed to get back to. No doubt she would learn, and very likely sooner rather than later. This woman was another familiar type, and Olympia recognized the pattern. She was a dropper of loaded phrases and leaver of pregnant pauses, hoping the listener would ask the obvious question she was hinting at. She'd met them and dealt with them before and no doubt would again. These people were needy, self-pitying and could be expertly manipulative. However, if the minister and the congregation could identify and attend to those needs, there was often a very nice person underneath, and everyone deserves a chance. This odd creature and her beautiful dog, in the right circumstances, could be an opportunity for growth and change on all sides. On the other hand, Olympia's new little church could be just one more stage to play out her little personal drama, and when the audience dried up or lost interest, she would pack up her dog and her tale of woe and move on. Time would tell.

Rayna and the dog stood up as one. "Would it be okay if I got Raggsy some water in the kitchen before we leave? It's hot out there, and I didn't bring any with me."

"I can't see why not," said Olympia. "Food for the hungry, water for the thirsty, two legs or four, that's my gospel, and I'm sticking to it."

When her little attempt at humor went unnoticed, she shifted to a more neutral tone. "I'm pretty sure Thelma and Selma will still be there. By the way, it was very nice of you to hop right in and give them a hand with the clean-up. People notice things like that, and those two notice everything. They won't leave until the last spot has been wiped clean. No doubt they can get you a dish."

"Thank you, Reverend Brown. See you next week."

"I'd like that." Olympia really meant those words. She wanted Rayna to come back next week and the week after that, as well.

CHAPTER 4

Out in the church kitchen the twins were in the finishing up stages after the coffee hour. Thelma was wiping down and polishing the faucets, and Selma was chasing down every last spot on the stainless steel work surface. "A gleaming kitchen is a happy kitchen," they would tell anyone who asked. Lest anyone forget, Selma had cross-stitched the not-so-gentle hint onto a piece of Irish linen. Thelma had it framed, and together they hung it in full view on the wall next to the sink. Woe betide the careless kitchen helper who didn't heed its warning.

The two were happily chattering, often finishing the other's sentences or talking over each other at an elevated volume, when Rayna Buxton and Raggsy approached the kitchen. Both women were becoming increasingly hard of hearing, and nobody but nobody ever dared mention it.

Thelma was stuffing the dishtowels into a carry bag

so she could bring them home to wash when Rayna and Raggsy came through the door.

"Well, then," said Thelma, "look who's here. It's our new kitchen aide." Then she laughed all over herself. "Get it? KitchenAid?" Selma picked up on the giggle. They made the same joke to every newcomer to their kitchen, and it never failed to make them chuckle. "Now, then, what can we do for you, my dear?"

"Well, I was hoping I could give my dog some water before I leave. It's getting really warm out there."

Thelma and Selma were temporarily lost for words. Water? Dog? Dog drips and dog splashes on their spotless floor? Neither of them spoke any of these words out loud, of course, but it was more than clear what they were thinking.

Rayna stood her ground. "I'm sure I can find a bowl in here somewhere, and I promise to wash it out and clean up any splash-over."

This put the twins between a rock and a hard place. To say no, especially to a visiting first-timer, would be un-Christian, unwelcoming and anti-dog. To say yes would mean that same dog would drink out of a bowl meant for humans and in so doing slop water and God knows what kind of dog germs on their pristine floor.

"I'll bring my own bowl next time, but just this once?" Rayna directed a head-bobbing, pleading smile at the two women, and after a fraction of a second it worked.

"Well, of course, dear," said Selma. "We love animals, don't we, Thelma? We had a bird once. It died. Here let me get you a nice big bowl, and when he's finished, I'll just take it home and wash it along with the dish towels."

"I'll wash it. I don't mean to be any trouble, and I really appreciate your doing this. I want to be able to come back here next week. Everyone's been so nice, you two ladies especially."

While Selma looked for and filled an acceptable bowl with cool fresh water, Thelma asked how Rayna and the dog were getting home, and did she need a lift?

"Oh, we'll just walk. It's not far. Walking's good for us. That's why I wanted the water. I didn't want Raggsy to get overheated."

"Well, what about you? You should have some water too."

"I can pick some up along the way. There's a convenience store near where I live."

"Nonsense." The twins spoke simultaneously. "There are always a few bottles in the fridge. You just take one or two of those."

"Only if I can replace them next Sunday."

"Oh, for goodness sake, girl, I think the church can afford to give you a couple of glasses of water, and if it can't, then we need to up our annual pledge!"

This made them all laugh, and Rayna reluctantly accepted the water and dropped it onto her tote bag. All the while Raggsy was making loud, messy work of finishing his own water while the twins were doing their best not to look at or listen to what was happening at their sensibly shod feet.

Rayna looked at the water on the floor, shook her head, and asked for some paper towels to clean it up.

"We use old cloth towels for the floor," said Selma.

"Paper towels are expensive and wasteful. We don't use them here." Thelma, handed Rayna a fresh, clean rag from the hand stitched rag bag hanging by the door.

"You just give it here when you're done," she held out her hand, "and I'll wash that along with the rest. You sure you don't want a ride home?"

Rayna shook her head. "Thanks again, ladies, but walking is good for me. It's not far, and I'll stick to the shady spots."

The twins didn't ask a third time. They smiled their goodbyes and told her they certainly could use her help again next week, but now she should probably run along, because they needed to have a word with Pastor Olympia.

Olympia, still sitting at the desk in the pastor's study, heard them coming. After only two encounters with them, she already recognized the unmistakable double beat of their footsteps. They came through the door in tandem, smiling in unison, and dropped as one into the two chairs opposite the desk.

"We talked to every member of the board during the social hour…" Thelma paused for dramatic effect but missed her moment, because Selma upstaged her and finished the sentence. "… and we are unanimous in wanting you to come and be our pastor. Aren't we, Thelma?"

It was not unexpected, and Olympia was genuinely pleased to be asked.

"I accept," she said, standing up and holding her arms out in an air-embrace. Then she added, "And before you leave, we will schedule a meeting to draw up that letter of agreement I described to you last week."

"Oh, dear, is that really necessary? We think you are just perfect in every way," said Selma.

"Just exactly what we need right now," finished Thelma.

Olympia held up her two hands in mock defense. "Hardly perfect, far from it, in fact, and yes, a letter of agreement is really necessary. In fact, I can't work without it. I need to know what is expected of me starting on day one. I'm sure you can understand. None of us likes to work in a void, never knowing what's coming next."

That they could understand and almost cheerfully told her they would call the board and then get back to her. The impromptu meeting was over.

After double-checking the lights and the locks on the windows, Thelma and Selma locked the outside door using their own key. Rayna, standing unseen in the shadows, watched them get into their car, a gleaming, vintage black Ford Crown Victoria, and drive slowly out of the parking lot.

When they were out of sight, she gave a gentle tug to the leash, and Raggsy instantly moved into position at her right side. The two walked across and out of the empty parking lot, turned left and, keeping to the patches of shade, continued down the tree-lined Main Street to an intersection where a small cluster of little shops were barely clinging to life. Many of these were mom-and-pop operations which had somehow managed to withstand the onslaught of Walmart and other manifestations of big box mania.

Among them, on the opposite corner, was a deli-convenience store and gas station combo that carried the Sunday paper and assorted sundries. It was owned and operated by a brown-skinned family from the Middle East. Rayna knew some people in town refused to do business with them because they were foreigners, and the women in the family wore headscarves to cover their hair. She had little time for such small-minded people and made it a point to learn to pronounce the owners' names and to stop in whenever she could. Now she stood on the corner, waiting for the light to change.

Inside the convenience store part of the operation, which always smelled vaguely of gasoline, Rayna wrinkled her nose, purchased a newspaper and a bag of taco chips and paid in cash. Once back outside, she pulled her cell phone out of the canvas tote bag and double-tapped on the Uber app. Ordinarily, she would have walked, but considering the heat, this was a necessity and not a luxury.

CHAPTER 5

Later that afternoon when Olympia got home, she found Frederick and the two cats sprawled under a tree in the back yard. Frederick opened one eye and raised an index finger in greeting. When it was that hot, no one expended any more energy than was minimally required. The cats didn't even twitch a whisker. To be sure, they did have room air conditioners in the bedroom and in the sitting room, but they were loud, and despite the comfort, Frederick complained that the air always smelled stale. He explained that he was English, and air conditioning was for less stalwart breeds. Olympia did not ask for clarification.

She looked at her watch. "Tea, my love?"

Frederick opened the other eye. "Believe it or not, my dear, I think not. As beloved a tradition as it surely is, it is hotter than bloody hell out here, and I think a glass of water would do very well."

"Well, since I'm already standing, I'll be happy to get it for you, but then I'm going back and plant myself directly in front of the AC and turn it up to Arctic Circle. I am getting too old for this kind of heat. I about died in that church this morning."

"Never use the word 'old,' my dear," Frederick got up out of his chair and was wiping the running sweat off his neck and chin. "Old is a matter of opinion. Perhaps 'seasoned' might be a better choice of words. Either way, much as I am opposed to air conditioners on principle, I do believe I'll join you in front of that infernal machine —not because I'm feeling the heat, you understand, but just to keep you company."

Olympia favored him with a well-practiced eye roll. "Hardly infernal, Frederick. In fact, one might actually say that it is the blessedly, diametrically and thermostatically polar opposite of infernal."

Inside the house he sprawled into the chair nearest the machine, his arms and legs flung out like an aging starfish, and groaned, "How the mighty have fallen. In England air conditioning is for sissies, for wimps. This is so unlike the home life of our own dear queen."

"Frederick?"

"Mmmm?"

"Do shut up."

<hr />

"HI, DEAR. BACK SO SOON? I MUST HAVE DOZED OFF. Still hot out there? How was church?" Rayna's mother's thin voice called out over the hiss of the air conditioner as her daughter came through the front door and into the living room.

"Hot and humid. Church was church. Same old, same old, but I suppose that's why I keep going. There are some things you don't want to change, do you? Church is one of them. You know, the comfort of the familiar. Do you want some iced tea while I'm up?"

"That would be lovely, dear, thank you. And a couple of cookies, maybe." The old woman looked childishly hopeful.

"Only if you promise to be a good girl."

"Oh, all right, if I have to."

It was their little joke, oft repeated because it made them both laugh.

Rayna leaned down to let Raggsy off the lead, kissed her mother on the top of her head and turned to go into the kitchen. The dog, in familiar territory now, sat down next to the lady in the recliner and thumped his head into her lap. It was all part of the routine. Whenever Rayna and the dog come home from an outing, Raggsy had to have a thorough head pat and ear scratch and then a doggie munchie from the stash she kept in her pocket.

Rayna returned with the tea and the plate of cookies and, after giving her mother her portion, flopped like a wilted rag doll onto the couch. "Thank God for AC," she reached for her tea. "Even the priest was sweating. Must be hot under all that finery, even with the AC. Too bad they don't have summer robes."

"What was the sermon about?"

"Same old, same old, different day, different gospel. I think it was about the Sermon on the Mount this time. To be honest, I wasn't paying that much attention. I guess I go because that's what I do on a Sunday morning."

"Well, I'm glad you've gone back. You were a long time away. I wish I could go, but I'm just not up to it, especially in this heat. Maybe someday."

"The Eucharistic minister still comes by, doesn't she?"

Her mother nodded and took a long swallow of her tea. "Her name's Betty Larkin. She comes on Wednesdays, but you're always away at work."

"I know. I set it up that way. It's a little company for you besides just the dog when I'm out at work."

"You still like working at the library?"

She shrugged her shoulders. "What's to like, what's not to like? It's only part time, but it's a job. I like books. It gets me out with people, which is good, but not too many, which is even better."

"You didn't used to be this way, you know."

Rayna lifted a wary eyebrow. "What way?"

"You not liking to be around people. You were such an outgoing little girl."

"Times change, people change. Don't worry about me, Ma. I've got you and Raggsy, a nice place to live and my church and my library. I'm good."

"What are you going to do this afternoon? We both know I'm going to have a little nap." She smiled sleepily.

"I'll probably go up to my room and work on my

scrapbooks for a while. Then if it cools down a little bit, I'll take Raggsy for a walk."

At the sound of his name, the intelligent dog lifted his head and looked at his mistress.

"Later, boy," she whispered. "Everything in good time. Are you going to stay here and guard Mama, or are you going to come upstairs with me?"

The dog lifted his head and appeared to think about this, and then, perhaps in hopeful anticipation of another treat, he grunted and once again dropped his head onto his paws.

THAT EVENING AFTER SUPPER, OLYMPIA CAUGHT HER cell phone as it was doing a little happy dance across the kitchen table. She usually kept it in vibrate mode so that a jangling ring would not interrupt what might be a pastoral moment. That, and she hated the sound of a telephone, any telephone, ringing. She lunged for and grabbed the little beastie before it kamikaze-d itself right off the table and onto the floor. It was not a number she recognized.

"Pastor Olympia?"

"Speaking."

"It's Rayna Buxton. I just wanted to thank you for being so nice to me today. You … well, everyone really … made me feel so welcome. I guess I'm not used to that. So thank you, and I will definitely come back next Sunday."

"Why, thank you, Rayna. Umm, was there anything else you wanted to talk about?"

"No. At least not now anyway. I don't want to bother you on a Sunday night when you must be all tired out. No, I just called to thank you."

CHAPTER 6

"Who was that, love?" Frederick was in the sitting room, resting off his supper.

"Just a woman who came to church this morning. Nothing I have to deal with tonight."

"Oh, that's all right then. Come in and sit down and take a load off your mind. It's nice and cool in here, and I want to hear all about your first day in the new church."

"As long as I'm out here, do you want coffee, tea or something stronger?"

"What are you having?"

"A large cold beer!"

"You don't usually drink beer."

Olympia was beginning to grind her teeth. "Frederick, just answer me. Do you want something or not? Speak now or forever hold your peace. I'm losing patience. I asked a simple question. It wasn't intended to be an inquisition or a debate."

"I'll have what you're having."

Olympia gave brief consideration to shaking the can she was holding like mad before tossing it to him, but her good angel intervened just in time. She handed the man a can and a glass before dropping into her favorite chair.

"You forgot a glass for yourself."

"I drink like a man." Olympia popped open her can, took a long noisy swig, and made a great show of wiping her mouth with the back of her arm before settling back and putting up her feet. "Ahhhhhhhhhh!"

"Your classic elegance never fails to charm me, but back to your day, good lady wife, do tell me the details."

Before she had a chance to begin her tale, the clock on the mantle *boinged* and almost simultaneously her cell phone buzzed, announcing another incoming call.

Frederick raised an eyebrow and pointed to the old clock while Olympia connected and then enthusiastically greeted her longtime "bestie," her priest-friend, Father Jim Sawicki.

"Hey there, Jim. How are you? How's Andrew? How's little Saint Sebastian, my nephew cat?" Frederick waved a greeting from his spot on the sofa. "Frederick says hi. When are we going to get together? It's been way too long."

Conversations with Jim were never lengthy. He never called just to chat, and while he was a man who lived by and preached The Word, he did not use words idly in his personal life. He'd called to arrange a visit.

In minutes they'd settled on what they'd come to refer to as a play date, an overnight trip into Boston so the four of them could kick back and relax with no parishioners watching. This time it was to be a visit to the air conditioned MFA, the Boston Museum of Fine Arts, dinner and an evening walk around Boston Common. After that would come a nightcap somewhere funky and a sleepover in a condo on Boston's Beacon Hill with Jim and his partner Andrew. Socializing with Jim and Andrew was always mid-week. She and Jim were both clergy and usually had Sunday duties. Andrew was a jazz musician, and like Jim worked mostly on weekends but at the other end of the day. Like so many musicians he was a night owl, but he and Jim had worked out a pattern that suited them.

"Now, then, where was I?" Olympia mused.

"You were going to tell me about your first day in the new church. Seems like everything is conspiring against that happening, though. Shall we give it one more shot or forget it and flip on the telly?"

She shook her head. "Not a lot to report. Way too early, and besides, first days anywhere are never the reality. Everybody has their party dresses on and is on their best behavior."

"Am I supposed to read something into that?"

She made a face. "I don't know yet, Frederick. It's a lovely old church in desperate need of repair with an aging, dwindling membership. They lose their long time pastor without warning. He had a massive stroke. They are grieving and disoriented, and they are hoping I can help them see a way forward—and oh, by the way, they hate change. They call themselves nondenominational, but they really mean nondenominational Christian. I'm not sure how they will deal with a Unitarian Universalist minister who sees Jesus as a good man who was of God but was not God himself. That's always a challenge. Oh, yes, and then there's the lady and the dog."

Frederick tipped his head to one side and looked at her over his beer.

"The lady and the dog? That sounds like the title of a Somerset Maugham short story."

She raised her beer can in mute acknowledgment. "A woman showed up in church with a service dog in tow. That's who just called. Clearly very needy, but I was really careful not to prejudge. I'm not used to having dogs in church. That could be my problem and no one else's. God knows I love animals, but they can be serious distractions. On the other hand, churches love to have someone or something to fuss over."

"Don't you mean fuss about?"

Olympia laughed. "We've been together too long, my love. Both, fuss *over* if they like you, and fuss *about* if they don't."

"So what did you do?"

"I welcomed them both, of course. It was a service dog. I have to say it was very well, actually perfectly, behaved, but something about her and the dog just made me a little uneasy."

"How so?"

"I'm not sure. Sixth sense maybe? Right now I think it's best to remain a cautious observer. I'm new there. The dog was perfectly trained, but I had the sense he could do some real damage if someone made the wrong move. There's a couple of little kids in that church. Little kids don't think, and they run at things."

Frederick frowned and rubbed his chin. "I see what you mean."

BOING! The clock was insistent.

"I guess she does, too," Olympia gave a nod of acknowledgement to the clock on the mantle. The clock they'd found in a secret place when they first bought the house. The clock that didn't work unless it had something to say. And when it did have something to say, they had learned to pay attention.

"So what do you think I should do?"

"I think you should sleep on it and say nothing. If there is a problem, let them be the ones to initiate the conversation. Who's in charge there? The board? The vestry? Parish committee? Wait and see what they think. It may not bother them at all."

"Spot on, my love. The last thing a new pastor does is bring up issues and point out problems on day one. That's a recipe for disaster, if I ever saw one."

"Of course, there is also the safety issue."

"Safety issue? I'm not sure I understand."

"If they do bring up the subject of the dog, and you feel some genuine concern, you do have every right to ask them whether a dog bite injury is a greater or lesser potential disaster than a contentious discussion with animal lovers on one side and the dog catchers on the other. But let them cast the first stone … or doggie treat."

Olympia held up both hands in surrender. "Of course, you're right, and I do thank you for being so." She shot him a mock sneer. "I would have gotten there in the end, but you just cut through the crap. I'm going to give it another week. She may not even come back. I've had that happen before, too. They come in, promise you the moon and never darken the door again. I'll give it a week, and if there is any noise at all, I'll pull a few heads together and address the situation."

CHAPTER 7

Ordinarily Olympia, like many clergy, took Mondays as her Sabbath, her own day of rest after working the weekend. Today, however, she decided it would be a good thing to take advantage of the one day a week in the summer schedule when she knew the church administrator would be in. She could introduce herself, have a private look around when the building would be virtually empty, and do a site inspection without interruption or an audience.

She'd learned long ago that the one person who could answer most of her questions about everybody and everything in virtually any church was the church administrator. Furthermore, she could look around, ask questions, maybe even make herself some coffee without benefit of the Fosselberg twins adding their genetically doubled two cents worth.

Mercifully, after a midnight thunderstorm, the weather outside had turned significantly cooler, and the

New England summer day was clear, bright and beautiful. After a leisurely breakfast with Frederick and the cats, Olympia poured her second cup of coffee into a travel mug, kissed her husband, patted each cat goodbye and stepped out into a beautiful morning. This was the life! One day she might think about retiring or maybe cutting back to part-time. The idea had wandered across her mind more than once in the last year, but she'd pushed it away. She still had a few good years of ministry left. This is what she was trained for. Comfort the afflicted and afflict the comfortable, each in its turn.

Inside the antique Brookfields farmhouse that had been their home for over a dozen years now, Frederick was having his second cup of tea and a little go at the daily crossword puzzle. He was happily anticipating a day at home. Alone. Much as he adored his lady wife, he needed time apart. They both did. His plan for the day was to continue working on the plans for his latest DIY home and garden project, a fish pond. The garden catalogs called such things "water features." Frederick loathed the term. It sounded so clinical. He'd had a back yard fish pond growing up in England. He knew that once you got it established, it basically looked after itself. He remembered having to drain it and scoop the fish poop off the bottom every couple of years, but how difficult was that? And the fish were like little pets. They even came to call, especially when the caller was holding a packet of fish food. He smiled at the happy childhood memory.

This was going to be a wonderful surprise for Olympia. The details of keeping secret the digging of a massive hole in the back garden, lining it with black plastic, and arranging a water source, not to mention the fish and the landscaping, had yet to be worked out. But details didn't bother Frederick. They never did. Things always had a way of working themselves out. He had the catalogs, he'd visited several local home and garden shops, looked up the how-to directions on line and even printed them out. Frederick was a man on a mission.

But first, extricate the crossword from underneath the cat and savor that second cup of tea.

CHAPTER 8

Olympia pulled into the church parking lot and parked her beloved blue VW van under the biggest tree she could find. Before getting out, she looked around and checked to see there was nothing of value anyone could possibly steal. There was not. She opened all the windows, slipped down from the high seat and headed toward the side entrance of the building. As she approached the office she called out a greeting to the church administrator, Becci McClain.

"Good morning, Pastor! I didn't expect to see you here. When we met last week you told me that you take Mondays off. Can't blame you there. You ministers work weekends when the rest of us don't. Whatever, come on in." Becci smiled broadly in welcome.

Olympia couldn't remember anyone in her middle-aged life appreciating how hard clergy worked and actually saying the words out loud. I think I'm going to like this woman, she thought.

"Ordinarily I do take Mondays off. In fact, I don't usually work much at all in the summertime. But when the offer came up, and I learned of the circumstances, I really couldn't say no. I thought about the difficulties and challenges you all must be experiencing over the loss of your former minister. I decided to start right away so I could get to know people and work my way in slowly. I hope I can be a stabilizing force as well as a comfort. So, here I am."

"And welcome as the flowers in May, I say, or in this case, in June." Becci smiled. "Pastor Dave's leaving was a terrible shock to everybody. I mean, we all know ministers eventually move on, but not like this. It happened with so little warning, and it was so debilitating, so final. Technically, he's still alive, but he might as well be dead."

The woman bit her lip and shook her head. "I mean the people here can't even visit him. The family wants no visitors." She paused. "On the other hand, he might not want any of us to see him in such a condition. I hadn't really thought of that. I wouldn't call him a vain man, but let's just say he was really good looking and paid careful attention to his appearance, if you know what I mean."

Olympia nodded in womanly understanding of the ways of male vanity. "So it was that bad, was it?"

Becci nodded and then added in a low voice, "Nobody would wish that on anyone." She paused and dropped her voice, "But just between you and me and the lamppost, I have to say there are a few here who are happy to see the last of him."

Olympia's invisible trouble-shooting antennae went

straight up. She cocked her head and looked at Becci. "Problems?"

She looked down at her desk and fiddled with the pencil she was holding. "Doesn't every church have its share? Personality issues and such. Let's just leave it at that."

Much as she wanted to know more, Olympia knew that day two of a new assignment was not the time to go anywhere near this, so she did the next best thing. She nodded sympathetically. "Anytime you get two or more people together in the same room, you'll likely have personality issues. Or politics. It's the way of the world." Then she gestured toward the pastor's office and changed the subject. "Actually, I probably won't be doing anything pastoral today so much as I'll be familiarizing myself with the building, and scratching around in the office. I'd like to clear out a little space in there and arrange things for myself. I won't throw anything out, but I will set up and arrange the desk in a way that works for me, maybe clear up a little of the clutter. He was here a long time."

"Good luck with that. The man was a pack rat. You'll probably find orders of service going all the way back to when he first came here." Again the quick tight smile. "After he had the stroke, his daughter came and took all his personal things, you know, family pictures, personal mementoes, old sermons and such." She held her two hands up and far apart. "It was really strange. The man hadn't seen his children in over ten years. The wife left and took them with her. I can only wonder what she thought."

Olympia filed that bit of information for future

reference and returned to the task at hand. She gestured to the pastor's study. "I am going to dig around in there, but I repeat, I won't throw out anything. There's probably a lot of church history in there."

Becci rolled her eyes. "More like a lot of junk, I'd say."

"You know what they say, one person's trash is another person's treasure. Besides which, the last thing a new minister does on day one is clean out all evidence of the old minister. We'll ask the board to take care of this. They can make the hard choices."

Any further conversation between Becci and Olympia was cut short by the creak of the outside door opening, and the unmistakable sound of the Fosselberg twins talking over each other as they marched toward the church office.

Becci rolled her eyes and chuckled. "Good luck to you. First day in the office, and you get the double whammy. And by the sound of them, this is not a casual morning drop-in."

"How can you tell?" whispered Olympia.

"Shall we just say I know a firm tread when I hear one. God bless them. They're the backbone of the church, and they pick every other bone they can find. I suspect it's about the dog yesterday."

"You heard about the dog already?"

"Small church, small town, Pastor. Why hello, Thelma, hello, Selma, lovely morning isn't it."

The two women smiled and nodded, and the flowers on their respective hats bobbed in unison. "It is a lovely morning, but if you don't mind, we've come to have a little chat with Pastor Olympia. Good morning, Pastor."

"We didn't really expect to find you here. You told us you didn't work on Mondays. So we were going to leave you a note. We don't use email. But then we saw your car and we just turned right in and here we all are."

Thelma pursed her lips and nodded her head, all the while the flowers on her hat responded to her every move.

"Well, then I guess we all got lucky didn't we." Olympia waved them in. "Do come in and sit down, ladies. It's nice and cool in there, and we can have a chat."

"I don't like air conditioning." said Thelma.

"Can we turn it off? It makes her sneeze."

Olympia opened the office door and stepped inside. "Actually, I don't think it's been turned on yet. There's a fan if we need it. Come on in. It's lovely and warm in here. You'll just love it."

The sarcasm of this was totally lost on the two Fosselbergs, but the church administrator, still seated at her desk, covered her mouth with both hands and convulsed in silent laughter.

Once they were inside the study, and all were seated, Thelma got straight to the point. "Reverend, I know we are supposed to welcome the stranger, but really, we've never had a dog come to church before. I'm not sure Jesus meant …"

"Well, there *was* Harold Dawson," Selma interrupted her sister. "You remember him. After he went blind he would bring his dog on Sundays. George, the dog's name was George. Nice dog. But the man was almost blind for Lord's sake. He needed that dog."

"Selma, don't interrupt me. I'm trying to get to the point. Reverend Olympia is a busy lady. She doesn't have all day to talk to us." *Translation: She'd better have all day if we feel we need it.* "Now then, where was I? Oh yes, the dog and that woman, Rayna was it? What are we going to do if she comes back?"

"Assuming she does come back," said Selma.

"Forewarned is forearmed," snapped Thelma, her color beginning to rise.

Olympia held out her hands, symbolically embracing the two ladies. "What do you think we should do?" She then folded her hands and looked up at the ceiling. She had never in her entire clerical career looked so thoroughly innocent.

"Well, isn't that your, job?" snapped Thelma. The lace gloves were coming off.

"Jesus tells us to welcome the stranger,"

"He didn't say anything about dogs."

"Birds of the air and beasts of the field, the most humble among us, his eye is on the sparrow. In my thinking that includes dogs. Trouble is, nowhere in the Bible, or the by-laws of this church, for that matter, does it give us directions on how to welcome what stranger." Olympia was bordering on pontification now, and she knew it. *Be careful woman! The last thing you want to do is alienate these good ladies. Their concern is genuine.*

Olympia decided to try a different approach. "To be honest with you, I've not really encountered this kind of thing before. I've had people come to church with seeing-eye dogs but never with a comfort dog. In fact, until yesterday I'd never even heard the term 'comfort dog.' I suppose it's much the same as a seeing-eye dog. So clearly the woman feels she needs the dog, uh, to be comfortable. So help me understand the problem."

Thelma and Selma were not prepared to have the question redirected back to them. "Well," Thelma paused, clearly looking for the words that would substantiate her argument. "Dogs are nice. Don't get me wrong."

"We even had one once. Daisy. She was a cocker spaniel. She bit everyone, so we had to get rid of her."

"Selma, please! Let me finish."

"It's just that dogs can be a distraction. It's hard to pray when a dog is panting or scratching, and the license tags are jingling."

"Did that happen this Sunday?"

"No, but it could."

"Rayna told me herself not to pat him without asking. We have children who come on Sundays. What if one of them ran up to the dog and got bitten. That would be just awful." Selma shook her head in distressful anticipation.

Olympia had had that selfsame concern, and now was not the time to share it, but there was no doubt that Thelma had a point.

"I have her contact information. I could call and ask that when she comes back she put a soft muzzle on the animal. That way she wouldn't have to worry about the dog getting protective, and nobody has to worry about getting nipped. What do you think, ladies?"

Two sets of shoulders relaxed, and the two ladies first glanced at each other and then smiled up at Olympia.

"Good idea, Reverend. Of course, I don't think we should have animals in church, but who am I to judge?"

Olympia did not believe that for a nanosecond. She continued, choosing her words carefully. "I do believe I'll go get a soft muzzle to have here at the church just in case Raggsy or another dog ever comes to visit. I think it would be good to have one on hand. Meanwhile, Rayna did tell me she was planning to come back next week, but lots of first-timers say that, and we never see them again.

Olympia made no mention of the telephone call she'd received from Rayna the evening before. "I would probably make a call anyway, just to make her welcome. That's just ministerial good manners. If she says she is planning to return, I'll suggest the muzzle. And if she forgets, I will have one here at the ready. How does that sound?"

"Why would someone need a comfort dog in the first place?" asked Selma.

Olympia framed her answer very carefully. "Probably for the same reason they have calming dogs at airports, in doctor's offices and in assisted care facilities and nursing homes. They help with anxiety. Science has proved that stroking an animal can actually lower your blood pressure. Did you know that?"

They didn't.

"Does that mean that Rayna has mental problems?"

Olympia held up both hands in the *back off* position. "No, it does not. It means exactly what she told us on Sunday. Raggsy helps her be out in the world. That's enough for me, and I hope it will be for you. Why don't we hold off on anything more until we see if she even comes back? If she does, thanks in large part to you two, we will do an even better job of welcoming her. Don't you think?"

If they didn't think so, they would never say, because neither one of them would be caught dead committing an un-Christian act. Repeat: *Caught,* in an un-Christian act.

CHAPTER 9

After thanking the Fosselberg twins for their time and concern and cheerfully blessing them on their ways of righteousness, Olympia turned to the self-imposed and delicate task at hand: moving into the former pastor's office. She'd done this any number of times before, and the trick was not to begin throwing things out but to start by looking around. This was not a cheerful task, especially because there was a real sense of sadness that went with it.

This man would not be going on to another ministry. He was done but not dead. Not blessedly and metaphorically passed away into a new life with the Lord but permanently shelved until such time as his stroke-ravished body could no longer sustain what was left of his life. What a sorry ending to a life dedicated to service.

Olympia knew she'd be clearing out the remnants of a ten-plus-year ministry. Beyond that was the sober reality that one day it would be her own things, her old sermons, family pictures of weddings and christenings, going into the boxes; and she, like all the others who have moved on to a "better place," would have no say in deciding where they went.

Olympia pushed away the thoughts of her own eventual demise, seated herself in the old swivel chair and set into the task at hand, and the file cabinet behind the desk. Anything to do with the church, orders of service, meeting minutes, files containing who knows what, she would have boxed up and saved for further action. She would ask the board to come in and decide which of the books remaining on the bookshelves belonged to the church and which should be sent to the local thrift shop. After that, when there was space, she would bring in a few of her own cherished favorites; pictures of the kids and now grandkids, the picture of her and Frederick on the day they were married, and the statue of Bastet, the Egyptian cat goddess Frederick had given to her on her sixtieth birthday.

Then there was the matter of the office furniture. She wrinkled her nose. The pastor's desk and chair were well used but still serviceable. Upon closer examination, Olympia could see that the desk was a relic from another age—heavy, ornately carved and inlaid and beautifully joined. The marks of its use bore witness to its years of service and in some ways, documenting the history of the church. She wondered if it had been commissioned and installed when the church was built. She would replace the well-worn seat cushion with one she could shape to her own comfortable contours.

The two visitor chairs were not in bad shape and still

comfortable, and other than needing a good cleaning, the oriental carpet, discolored in spots by the sun, was still quite lovely. Faded elegance.

The curtains were in need of a wash, and so were the windows, but most of this was cosmetic and should not raise any eyebrows or feathers when it happened. Olympia knew the drill: Make very small changes, and make them very very slowly.

With the quick assessment finished, she stood and picked up the seat cushion with her thumb and forefinger and dropped it onto one of the visitor chairs. The chair responded with a puff of dust. Olympia made a mental note to vacuum and air out every inch of the place. That could begin immediately.

With a soft grunt she pushed open the two windows as wide as she could, and filled her lungs full of clean fresh air before sitting back down at the desk. She'd been putting this bit off, going through the desk drawers, because she really didn't like going through another person's things. The poor man wasn't dead, but he was permanently out of action. She took a quick breath and pulled open the middle drawer

Not surprisingly, in the sectioned tray at the front she found the familiar assortment of pencils, pens, rubber bands, sticks of chewing gum, paper clips and sticky notes, some with words scribbled on and some blank and at the ready. Behind that, deeper into the drawer space were more pens, a rock hard granola bar, a three-year-old appointment calendar and a small assortment of greeting cards and personal thank you notes. Poignant really. A sweet-sad personal picture of a minister's working life. It was not unlike her own. Who was this man? What was he really like? And if he was such a lovely man, then why did his wife leave him and take the children with her?

These thoughts and others like them collected at the edges of her thinking as she fingered the objects before her. The little sectioned tray at the front of the drawer, smooth and pleasant to the touch, on second inspection was not quite centered. Something underneath it, most likely an escaped pen or pencil, was preventing it from sitting flat on the surface beneath it and fitting flush against the front of the drawer.

Because she liked things to fit where they are supposed to, Olympia pushed and pulled and eventually pried the tray out of the drawer and discovered what was causing the irregularity. There in the center drawer within easy reach were two unused condoms, one empty condom packet and an envelope containing a very explicit photograph.

"Damhellshitcrap." Olympia whispered. She could feel her pulse quicken and her blood pressure rise. "What the hell do I do now?" Then she answered her own question. "I touch nothing. I say absolutely nothing. I replace the tray, and I call Jim right this very minute."

Olympia pushed the drawer back in with the end of a pencil, stood up and went into the outer office.

"Were you talking to someone on the phone? I didn't hear it ring." Becci looked up from her computer.

"Just muttering to myself. Say, I'm going out for a breath of air and some coffee; can I bring you one back?" Olympia prayed she didn't look and sound as shaken as she truly was.

"No, thanks, too hot for coffee. I have some iced tea." Becci shook a tall plastic container. "If anyone calls, can I say when you'll be back, or should I just take a message?"

Olympia had to think about that. "I won't be long. It's dusty in there, and I just need a little break and some fresh air. I'll be back. Half, three-quarters of an hour maybe. You sure you don't want anything? Dry martini?"

Becci laughed and waved her off. "You are a hoot. Go on then."

Olympia often resorted to humor when she found herself in an awkward situation, or in this case, caught on the horns of a dilemma—a really awkward professional, ethical and personal dilemma.

Olympia walked over to a shady spot under a massive maple tree that shadowed much of the church parking lot. There, leaning on the mottled trunk for comfort as well as for support, she called Jim. Father Jim, her best friend forever. He was an openly gay ex-Catholic priest, now Anglican priest, living in a committed relationship with Andrew Saunders, a jazz pianist from Jamaica.

When he answered, she wasted no time in getting to the point. "Hey, Padre, got a few minutes? I need some advice."

"Is this five minutes' worth of advice or two hours of clerical confidence advice?"

"Probably both. Church issue. Possibly a very bad one.

"As Hershel, my rabbi friend, would say, *oy gevalt* already. Let me guess. You started work at the new church and discovered the treasurer is having an affair with the choir director, and the administrator is embezzling money from the endowment, and a hungry feral cat has a litter of kittens in the tool shed, and you brought them all home."

"Not far off—well, at least not the kittens anyway—and it's not funny. I'm serious. I need help. I'll give you the five-minute version now, and then we can decide if I or we need more time."

Jim was instantly serious. "Sorry, Olympia."

"It's okay, Jim. You couldn't have known."

"What's going on?"

"I came in this morning to have a look around the office. You know, clear out the old and make a space for myself. I was poking around in the pastor's desk, and found two packets of condoms plus an empty wrapper and right next to them, an envelope containing a porno-graphic photograph. It was nauseating, and I don't think he was keeping the things for a friend."

"Oh, shit." Jim was not given to swearing unless it was absolutely necessary. "What did you do?"

"I closed the drawer, walked out into the parking lot and called you."

"This is not a parking lot conversation. Any indica-tion of clergy misconduct that you can see or sense?"

"Not on day two, Jim. There was the occasional awkward silence and sideways glance when I asked ques-tions about his pastoral care, but they don't know me. They're still testing the waters. They're not going to say anything to me yet. I'm still an outsider."

"Here's what I would suggest. You're new there. New ministers in a church or parish usually make an effort to get to know the congregation, one person or family at a time. Start asking questions, my friend, lots of very discreet questions and take careful notes."

"And there's another thing."

"Good lord, Olympia, you don't do anything by halves do you? Go ahead, let go of the other shoe."

"A woman brought her dog to church yesterday."

"Was the dog a problem?"

"No. Both lady and dog were very well behaved. It was a service dog, but it still upset a couple of the older members. The woman seemed anxious and pretty needy, but that's probably why she had the dog."

"No brainer, Olympia. Needy lady with a dog *vs.* credible evidence of possible sexual misconduct in the minister's study? Make friends with the dog, be nice to the owner of the dog and start asking questions about the minister."

"Thanks Jim ... I think."

"You've got your work cut out for you this time, Olympia. And I warn you, be careful. These things most often blow up in the face of the immediate successor. You will be trying to help a group of people who either don't know they need help or do know and never ever under any circumstances at all want to talk about it or admit that it happened on their watch. If it is true, and he wasn't keeping the condoms in his desk for a friend, there are going to be land-mines all over the place. Don't step on one. Call me when you get home tonight, and we'll decide when to meet for a CCC."

"What's that?"

"Confidential Collegial Coffee."

"I love you, Jim. Talk to you tonight."

CHAPTER 10

Olympia smiled, dropped the phone into her slacks pocket and headed back into the church and straight into Becci's office.

"I'm back! It's so close to lunch time that I decided all I really needed was some fresh air. That office needs a serious airing," she laughed. "Maybe we could rent an extractor fan. That'll get the job done in a hurry. My husband has one is his workshop. It really works, and I'm babbling."

She paused more for effect than to catch her breath. "When I was standing out there under the tree, I got the idea that maybe we could go grab a bite together and get acquainted. I'm sure you know of somewhere we can have lunch around here that isn't a fast food place."

"I do indeed. It's called The Green Onion. It's a vegetarian place, but the food is great. I go there all the time. It's about a ten-minute walk from here."

"Well, fancy that, I'm vegetarian. How convenient is that?"

Becci flashed a thumbs up in Olympias direction. "Well, that's one thing we have in common. I am, too."

"Is it a new place then?"

"The building used to be a shoe factory. Like in so many places around here, where the factories closed, the empty buildings just sat there and collected dust, mice and squatters until someone saw the potential and started repurposing them. Then the Department of Transportation extended the commuter rail. Now the little town of South River is on a definite economic upswing, which of course is a mixed blessing."

"How so?"

"Gentrification, Pastor. Properties bought on the cheap and condo-ized or repurposed and resold, means poor people who live here can't afford them. The nature and character of the town is changing. You'll see it happening in the church, if you stay that long. Older families are selling off their houses for quick money and then can't find a place they can afford in their own home town, so they move elsewhere. The people who are moving in have more money, and they want more trendy amenities, like The Green Onion, for example. Terrific food but at a cost, and that's a story for another time. The food's great, and the décor is funky. You'll love it."

"So what are we waiting for? Lead on, my friend."

Becci collected her purse and sunglasses and then walked over to the door to the pastor's study, pulled out a key and started to lock it.

Olympia held up her hand. "Oh, don't bother with

that. I do have to close the windows, but I'm not a door locker. There's nothing anyone would want in there. Pastor Dave's personal things are all gone, and I haven't brought anything of my own in yet. I was just getting the lay of the land."

"Force of habit. He always locked it. So help me God, I think he even locked it when he went to use the bathroom. I just figured it was one of his little oddities, and it certainly didn't make any difference to me. I'm just the paid help." She held up both hands and shrugged her shoulders. "We all have our quirks. He was a privacy freak, and if you think about it, that's a good thing. He would tell you he was always very respectful of people's privacy and confidentiality."

I'll just bet he was, thought Olympia, *and you can bet your bottom dollar I'm going to look into that very thing.*

"Pastor? You ready?"

Olympia blinked. "Sorry, my mind wandered for a second. I'm ready, and I'm hungry."

The Green Onion was a small place. Its mismatched secondhand store, shabby-chic tables and chairs were closer together than Olympia would have preferred, but on the other hand it was informal and cozy. The place was one of those exposed brick, high ceilinged, uneven oiled floor, converted factory spaces that were favored by the kinds of people who would open a vegetarian restaurant. It totally looked the part. Next to it was a yarn shop, a "Sheep to Shawl" establishment with yarns and spinning wheels and looms arranged in such a way that invited closer observation and conversation. It smelled like lanolin. Olympia made a promise to self to come back alone or with Frederick and have a thorough off-the-clock meander around the place. Anyone who knits can always use more yarn.

The only available table was against the wall opposite a coffee machine with so many tubes and handles and flashing lights that it looked and sounded like a blast furnace. Noisy. The upside was that no one on God's green earth, even someone sitting at the next table could hear them.

Over their jelly jars of carrot and apple juice, salads of mixed greens and grains, and slices of homemade Anadama bread with freshly churned butter, they talked about where they grew up, their families and their work history.

Later over triple filtered, dry roasted over a wood fire, organically grown, free-range coffee to accompany their oversized, sweetened with local honey, non GMO oatmeal and raisin cookies, Olympia carefully got down to business.

"So, Becci, not to be nosy or gossipy, but more for clarification and understanding, can you tell me a little bit about the shoes I'm filling here? What was Pastor Dave like as a minister?"

She looked perplexed. "I'm not sure I understand. I mean, he was here for over ten years, so that in itself speaks volumes."

"I guess I'm asking if he was more of a pulpit pastor or more of a low key pastoral man. Was he interested in social justice, family ministry, youth outreach, pastoral counseling, all of the above? Youth ministry? I'm not snooping. I'm asking how he did his work and what took up most of his time. That way I'll know what particular pieces of the job I'll need to pick up first. We both know the church administrator knows all, sees all and usually says nothing. You're part of the team. At least that's how I see it. Right now, I'm trying to understand how you, in your opinion, see how the ministry of this church works. Needless to say, I'm going to ask other members of the congregation, as well. It's all part of the settling in process. It will help me do my job."

"Okay, now I understand," Becci nodded. "Pastor Dave was a good preacher. That alone brought in a lot of new people. Some of us thought he went on too long, but isn't that true everywhere?" She rolled her eyes, chuckling at her own little joke and went on. "I guess you could say he was his own man. He was super friendly. He welcomed everybody with a hug, even the men." She paused. "I kept the church calendar, so I know he did a lot of home visits, especially when a family or a person in that family was in need. You know, like a death or illness or divorce. He did beautiful funerals. I guess it sounds weird to say it, but everyone loved his funerals."

"Not at all," said Olympia. "I do a pretty good funeral myself, and I'm not bragging when I say it. I take the time necessary and put my heart and soul into it. It's the one thing I can do when there's nothing anyone else can do. Actually, I feel honored when I'm asked to do a funeral. It's a very precious time."

"Wow, I never thought of it that way."

"Once again, remember I'm not prying but more like trying to create a job description for myself. Were there any problems, underlying or out in the open that you know of?"

She laughed. "Well, if you mean who has control of the kitchen and who does the flowers for the altar on Sunday, we all know it's the Fosselberg twins. We couldn't function without them, but they *are* a mixed blessing. There can be little tensions around that sometimes."

Olympia held up both hands in acknowledgment. "Every church has them. Behind closed doors we call them 'the ladies who make the coffee.' They are a blessing but one that needs regular attention." And then she gently changed direction.

"I can see that attendance has been slowly dropping here, but that's true everywhere. Demographics change, people move, needs change, or people simply have too much to do, and church is the first thing to fall off the plate. You've been here for over ten years, from before Pastor Dave came. I wondered if you had any thoughts on that trend with regards to South River Community Church."

Becci paused for only the barest fraction of a second before saying, "No, not really, nothing I can think of."

It was only a moment, but the micro-hesitation was enough to tell an experienced minister that the woman had something more to say, and she wasn't about to say it —at least not now. Olympia packed that observation away for further reference and returned to more neutral questions about the history of the South River community itself and how developers were moving in and making use of the abandoned factories and what it was doing to the fabric of the community.

When they were finished, Olympia insisted on paying the bill, and before they actually started back, she dragged Becci into the Sheep-to-Shawl shop and begged a few empty boxes.

"I'll be cleaning out the desk in the study and I'm going to need these. I'll pack up anything that should stay with the church in one of them and anything I think can be tossed out in the other for the board to make the final call. I learned the hard way never ever throw anything away without asking."

After that the two women, each carrying a couple of nested boxes, walked back to the church. It was a beautiful day, and they took their time, stopping to admire gardens, converse with a neighborhood cat, and all the while, Olympia listened and learned more and more about a community and a congregation in transition.

When they got back they deposited their boxes on the floor of the study, and Olympia asked, "How much longer will you be working today?"

"About another hour or so. There's not all that much do in the summertime. Why?"

"I thought I'd stay on for a while and try and make some more headway in the clearing out process, but I make it a habit not to be in a church building without someone else present."

To Becci's questioning look, Olympia said only, "There was an incident. It was a few years ago now. A woman was stalking me, and she caught me alone in an empty building."

"A woman?"

"It's a long story. I'll tell you sometime. It all worked

out in the end."

"In that case, I don't blame you, but if you do decide to stay on today, I'll show you how to bolt the door from the inside. Even people with a key will have to ring the bell to get in."

"Okay, then, give me a heads up when you get ready to leave, will you?"

"Sure thing, Pastor."

Olympia turned into the study and left the door standing open. She felt like a stranger in a strange land. It was the pastor's study, but had it also been a place of assignation? Or worse? There was a lot of cleaning up to do, and it wasn't just the dust. Go slowly and take careful note of everything, she told herself, and maybe even take pictures while you're at it. There are some serious land-mines here, and you may or may not be able to defuse them. But neither can you look the other way and pretend they don't exist.

"Why me?" she whispered into the room full of secrets.

Because you can, and you will.

"Damn," said the Rev. Dr. Olympia Brown, and she didn't care who heard her. She had already known the answer.

"You say something, Pastor?"

"Scram…I was talking to the dust."

Olympia only wished she was. She took out her phone, pulled open the middle drawer, lifted out the removable pencil tray and snapped several pictures of the condom packets and the torn empty wrapper…and finally, the photograph.

CHAPTER 11

A few miles north of South River, Frederick was humming something from Gilbert and Sullivan's *Pirates of Penzance* and bumping along in his yellow 1952 Ford pickup. He was on his way to the home and garden store. He had his little list. He had his design, carefully drawn to scale on graph paper inside a folder marked WG, and he had his credit card. He was a man on a mission. He was going to create a water garden for his lady love. Over the course of the morning, the idea of a simple whiskey barrel fish pond had expanded and morphed itself into a creation that was combination of Monet's garden and the gardens of Versailles. He stubbornly refused even to use the expression, "water feature." That trendy term sounded so clinical, The words "water garden" conjured up visions of waterfalls, of flashing fish and happy little frogs, of aquatic plants and circulating pumps all using God's own free, precious rainwater that he alone would soon direct from rooftop gutters down and away to his own little garden of Eden.

Even if Adam and Eve didn't have such modern conveniences as running water in their garden, Frederick, being a man of his time, would have it in his, and God, being of a more universal and eternal time, would provide it.

SEVERAL BLOCKS AWAY RAYNA BUXTON WAS SITTING at a long oak table in the reference room at the back of the town library. Her task of the morning was an ongoing one. When she wasn't looking something up for a patron or shelving books or dusting the shelves themselves, Rayna cleaned up and repaired damaged books. Her job was to go through the books one by one, find and erase pencil marks, unfold corners and repair tears. Over the years she'd gotten very good at this, so good that the library paid for her to take a book and document restoration course and now were well rewarded for their efforts. When Rayna found a book that was damaged beyond repair, she took it to the head librarian, who would make the decision to replace it or simply remove it from the collection. Sometimes these books would be put into the annual Friends of the Library book sale, but when the damage was too great, or the book seriously out of date, the tattered victim of age and constant use would be consigned to the dumpster. Then, quietly and without fanfare, many of them made their way to the bottom of Rayna's canvas tote and then home to be added to her own expanding collection.

It was a perfect situation. The money was enough to supplement her mother's pension. The job got her out of the house on a regular basis, and because it was part-time, it left her plenty of time to care for her mother and Raggsy. It also gave her ample time and opportunity to pursue her own interests when no one was looking. Under the appearance of repairing a book, Rayna was able to do her own research, often taking a book home and then, dutifully and unobserved, quietly replacing it the next day. Sometimes, using a scalpel-sharp X-ACTO knife, she carefully and expertly sliced out whole pages for use in her scrap books.

She looked down at her watch. Almost quitting time. She'd left a sandwich on a plate in the fridge for her mother. She knew the dog was okay for another couple of hours, and it was beautiful outside. The idea of grabbing an ice cream for lunch and walking across town to see if the church was open appealed to her. Even if the building wasn't open, she'd take a walk around the outside and further check out the neighborhood. Maybe that new pastor would be in. Rayna hoped she would be. If she was, they could have another chat—a longer one this time.

BECCI CALLED FROM THE OUTER OFFICE, "I'M GETTING ready to leave now, Pastor. Do you want to come see how to deadbolt the door from the inside?"

It took a minute for Olympia to realize she was being spoken to. She hadn't fully adjusted to being called Pastor. She'd always been Reverend or the more casual and intimate Rev. in all of her other churches.

"Hang on, I'll be right there."

CHAPTER 12

When Becci was out and on her way home, and the two outside doors securely locked, Olympia returned to the pastor's study to contemplate in privacy that which she'd uncovered earlier that day. Where there's smoke, there's fire, she thought and wondered with a sense of dark foreboding what else might turn up now that she was alone and unobserved.

But locks or no locks, the first order of the afternoon was to open the windows back up and get some natural light and fresh air in the place. Once she could see and breathe she could make some progress.

The first and most obvious hiding place is always the far back of the bottom drawer on the left side—the left side because so many people are right handed, and getting into the left one is more difficult. Therefore it's less likely to be searched first, if at all. That and the right-hand bottom drawer, which had held Pastor Dave's sermons and personal writings, had been cleared out by the family.

With one of the empty boxes on the floor beside her, Olympia swung around on her chair and pulled open the drawer, which was filled with labeled and dated manila folders. Upon closer inspection over half of them appeared to be financial and attendance records dating from ten years back to the present. There were a few others labeled Christmas Sermons-Reference-Reflections. The family must have missed these, she thought, and made a mental note to keep them. But Olympia was on a dark mission, and working on the theory that appearances can be deceiving, she lifted the entire contents out of the drawer and spread everything out on her desk.

In some ways she was mildly disappointed to find they were, in fact, nothing more than old financial and attendance records, a couple of misfiled insurance forms and a folder containing newspaper clippings and more past Christmas sermons.

It was only when she dived into the drawer a second time to pull out two folders which had somehow gotten lodged way at the back under the others did she find the folder that confirmed her worst suspicions. It would appear that Pastor Dave had made and kept a collection of photographs starring himself and a variety of female partners engaged in what could only be described as fleshly pleasures. Women who, by the look of them, were not playboy models but unvarnished, un-Photoshop-ed ladies who looked like they could live next door or down the street. Someone you'd meet in the grocery store. Who were these women, and how in God's name did their salacious and compromising pictures end up in the bottom drawer of Pastor Dave's desk, the same desk where he kept packets of condoms and tossed the wrappers? The folders were labeled Reference Material. What in hell was he referencing? And all of this in a room that could be locked and shaded from the inside? Olympia propped her elbows on the desk, dropped her head into her hands and tried to compose herself. She was actually shaking and feared she might be ill when a voice came through the open window.

"Hi, Pastor, can I come in? I mean, only if you have time. I can always come back some other time."

Olympia flew out of her seat as though she'd been shot.

It was Rayna, floppy hat and all, standing outside the window looking in and waving timidly. Her first agonizing thought was, had Rayna seen anything? But one look at Rayna's angle of vision told her the filthy secret was safe for now.Breathe, Olympia. Act normal, whatever that might be under present circumstances!

"Hi, Rayna. I wasn't expecting you." *Gulp.* "How nice to see you. Go on around to the main door. Give me two minutes to clear off my desk, and I'll come and let you in."

"Thank you, Pastor. I didn't mean to startle you. I'm sorry. I didn't know if you'd be here, but I saw your car so I decided to take a chance. The door was locked, so I came around to the back to check and saw you through the window."

"I startle easily. Don't give it a second thought. You go on around to the door, and I'll be right there."

Olympia scooped up the old church files and set them into the box marked "old files" at her feet. The two "personal" files she shoved deep into her own carry bag and hastily covered them with a handful of old church newsletters.

Moments later she slid back the deadbolt and opened the door to an apologetic looking woman in an oversized sun hat and no dog.

"Where's Raggsy?" said Olympia.

"He's home. Each day I try and go a little farther without him. Some days I can and other days I can't. It's hard, but I'm getting there. You know, baby steps." Rayna flashed a weak and ingratiating smile that was more grimace than grin and ducked her head.

"Well, it's good to see you trying like this, Rayna. Come on in. I'll be honest, I don't have a lot of time left today but certainly enough for a cup of coffee or some iced tea. Can I interest you in some?"

"Oh, I don't have to stay. I mean, if you're busy ..."

Olympia knew what she really meant was, *you probably really don't want me here, but please try and convince me that you do.* She'd played this little push you-pull me game so many times. Rayna would grow to trust her or she wouldn't, but Olympia would do her pastoral best to see that she one day could.

"No no, come on in. I was ready for a break myself, and you've given me the perfect reason to take it. So thank you, and let's go straight out into the kitchen."

Once they were in the kitchen, Rayna positioned

herself so she could lean against the counter next to the stove and watch while Olympia lifted two glasses out of one of the wall cupboards.

"Now, then, what can I get for you?"

"Just water. I don't want to be a bother."

"Perfect. I'll have some too. Would you like some ice?"

"Only if it's not any trouble."

Olympia quietly ground her teeth.

"Two glasses of water with ice coming up." Olympia held up the glasses. "Tell you what, let's go and sit in the church parlor. It's a little neater in there. I'm doing a bit of housekeeping in the study, and it's a bit cluttered right now."

The room was airless and hot but at least there was nothing troublesome or incriminating in evidence. Olympia pushed opened the windows and sat opposite her surprise visitor. Inside, she was mentally drumming her fingers and wiggling her foot in exasperation at the ill-timed interruption, but to all outward appearances she was the perfect non-anxious pastoral presence. And that's what counted.

"Well then, Rayna, you told me it's been a good day and I'm pleased to hear that. Why don't you tell me what makes a good day for you, then maybe we can think about ways for you to have more of them?"

CHAPTER 13

Frederick was already home and sitting in a lawn chair, enjoying a cold drink under the massive oak tree that would one day cast its dappled shade over his still developing water garden. All evidence of his landscaping plans and explorations were carefully hidden from view, and he and the cats were the picture of bliss and innocent domesticity when Olympia crunched up the gravel drive to a stop outside the kitchen door. He waved in greeting, and when the motor stopped, both cats ambled over to meet their mistress.

"What-ho, my love? How was day two on the new job?"

"Complicated. I'll tell you when I get changed." She paused. "Um, this may be a stupid question, but how come you are not sitting in there," she pointed, "and enjoying the new conservatory? You worked your tail off to get it finished. Let's go in and enjoy it."

"Oh, um, well you see, I was, uh, thinking about

setting up a little shade garden under the tree here. So I was just sitting here and feeling the space."

Mine is not to reason why, thought Olympia. "Let me go get into a pair of shorts and a tee-shirt, and I'll join you and tell you about my day. Jim hasn't called, has he? My phone rang in the car, but I didn't answer it."

"Good for you for not answering it, and yes, he did call. He and Andrew are coming down this evening. They are bringing dinner. We didn't have anything on for tonight, did we?" He flashed her a weak smile.

As it was in many, if not most, families, Olympia maintained the family appointment calendar, and her husband paid little attention to it other than to ask what he was doing that day. Most of the time the arrangement worked, but when it didn't, it failed spectacularly.

As luck would have it, they had no outside plans, no theater tickets and no reservations. Olympia had planned a night off from cooking and was counting on leftovers supplemented by a past-its-sell-by date box of mac and cheese if needed to do the job. With Jim coming they would eat well—fabulously, in fact. Jim was a gourmet. He was a food and wine snob, and he loved to cook. For good reason he was one of Olympia's and Frederick's most favored dinner guests.

Within minutes she was back with her husband, under the tree with yet another glass of iced tea, her third that day, wearing an old tee shirt and a pair of knee-length khaki drawstring shorts. Baggy chic, she called them. It was her at-home summer outfit, never to be seen beyond the boundaries of her own plot of land.

Frederick held up his glass in salute, and she dropped into the chair opposite him. "No wine?"

"Jim will be bringing wine tonight, and if I start now, I'll be pie-eyed by the salad course. I want to enjoy supper and not sleep through it."

"So how did today go? I have to say, you are looking a bit strained around the edges."

"That obvious, is it?"

"Not to the casual observer, my love, but I do know you a bit more intimately than do the others." He followed his husbandly observation with a lascivious wink.

"Thank God for small favors."

"Small?"

"Favors, Frederick, and many of them most welcome and relished favors. Now do you want to hear about my day or not?"

"I do."

"I'll give you the short form, because I'll be saying it all again when Jim comes tonight."

Frederick frowned. "This sounds serious, Olympia. The lady with the dog, chapter two?"

"I only wish. As a matter of fact, the lady with the dog did come back today, but she just wants attention and reassurance. She's working her way back after chemotherapy for breast cancer. She suffers from anxiety and depression, and she's caring for an aging parent. She has every right to be anxious. I just have to be careful to not let her become too dependent on me. People like that can glom onto you, hang on for dear life and get really nasty if you try and disengage them. Remember that poor woman in the church on the Cape?"

"The one that swan-dived out of the choir loft and damn near killed herself?"

Olympia nodded. "That's the one. Rayna is nowhere near as bad as that. She just has a lot on her plate, and she doesn't have great coping skills. I'll spend some time with her, make my own assessment, and, if necessary, make some recommendations for counseling. I've learned not to take people like her on myself. People with serious boundary issues can get overly dependent fast—but my major concern is not about her."

"Dear God, woman, you mean there's more?"

"There is indeed." She told him in enough detail that he understood why she looked so discomforted and then added, "And I have the pictures right here with me."

He held up his hand in the stop gesture. "I don't want to see them, and I wish that you hadn't."

"I wish I hadn't either, but I did. My guess is that he's been systematically abusing women in the congregation, secretly photographing his escapades and then using them as evidence to guarantee silence and compliance."

Frederic grimaced in disgust. "Nice fellow. He's had a stroke, right? Well, at least he can't hurt anyone else, but that's not the point. It happened, and you have the proof. What are you going to do?"

She shook her head. "No effing idea, my love. That's why I desperately need to talk with Jim. I need to talk to a colleague. The abusing minister is medically out of commission. He had a stroke, he can't walk, and from what I hear, he can barely even talk. He's not going to do this again. But there are God-knows-how-many women out there, or more likely right around here, that he's abused and taken advantage of."

"So how can Jim help beyond being a sounding board? Are you going to tell anyone what you found?"

"That, my love, is the million dollar question. Right nowI have no idea what to do. That's why I need to talk to Jim. There are probably some people in the congregation who know or at least have strong suspicions about what happened. Some of the victims may even still be there or live nearby."

"Is there an argument for letting sleeping dogs lie?"

"Years ago there might have been, but not any longer."

Frederick looked perplexed. "I am not being intentionally obtuse, my darling, but some things are just better left untouched. Opening up old wounds could have devastating effects on the victims, as well as their families. Are you sure you want to—or should—carry this any further?"

"I don't want to, Frederick, but I do have to. I can't stay silent. That's how these things continue to happen, and despicable bastards like Pastor David Edward Cameron get away with what they do. It's a dark, conspiratorial web of lies, silence and complicity. In addition to the abused women, this kind of thing can poison a church for generations. The dark secret that everybody knows about, no one will talk about and that keeps on poisoning the very air around them."

Frederick dropped his chin and looked over the top of his glasses at his wife.

"I'm sorry you have to deal with this."

Olympia returned the gaze. "Me, too."

As if to change the subject, Cadeau, the sleek black cat Frederick had given to her as a Christmas gift some years ago, bolted out from under her chair and scrabbled up the tree after a squirrel. He never caught the squirrels, nor did he ever lose hope. Squirrels were for chasing. It was part of his genetic history.

They both laughed. Some things never changed.

June 1868

Lovely weather today. The children can't seem to get enough of it. My Jonathan, Susan's Lucinda, and now, Lottie's daughter Emmalee, are like little mud-scarps, little wild things, ducking and dodging in complete abandon through the woods and fields. This is as it should be when you are a child. But a cloud of suspicion is growing around our patchwork little family, and it is beginning to affect the very air we breathe.

It all started when Susan and I, in order to keep`` ourselves occupied and to put flesh on the bones of our convictions, made the decision to open a school for girls, both white and negro, daughters of white townspeople and daughters of freemen and freed slaves, in the belief that girls and young women are underserved in this supposed land of the free and the brave. We hold the belief that women can be more than homemakers and domestic *servants, but if that is to become a reality, they must first be literate.*

Very shortly after we stated the nature of the school we wanted to establish we became aware of a growing resistance to such an idea. Had I not been an avid follower of the works and writings of Olympia Brown, a determined advocate of women's right to education and the right to vote, I might have succumbed to the mounting arguments to desist in our efforts. Alas, these people do not know me as well as they think. Their resistance only fuels my insistence.

But I fear there is another cloud building on the far horizon, a darker web of lies and suspicions designed to tarnish and possibly destroy my good name.

More anon.

LFW

CHAPTER 14

Several hours and even more miles away from the towns of Brookfields and South River, inside the community room at The Birchwood, an assisted living and life care community, Pastor David Edward Cameron had been moved to what would be his next-to-last resting place. He was parked near the others facing an oversized, high-volume television set. He sat, leaning sharply to the left in a motorized wheel chair, in the company of the few residents, who, with enormous and respectful assistance, were still marginally mobile. This meant they were not totally bedridden and certainly benefitted from being moved out of their rooms to where they could socialize. Nobody ever explained how this was actually possible when the speech, hearing and vision of most of the residents was seriously impaired, but certainly proximity alone, being in sight of another human face, had to be a contributing factor to their wellbeing.

The dedicated staff of this five-star establishment knew full well how important it was to keep the residents involved and integrated and active for as long as they could. They understood that a man with a still sound-mind in a failed body needed more than good food and regular bowel movements to have anything that resembled a meaningful life. To that end, they made a genuine effort to create a community within a community, using book groups, chair yoga classes, a chess club and even a choral singing group. It had been medically proven that music, played or just even listened to, could soothe the savage breast of Alzheimer's and lighten the gloomiest day, if even for only short periods of time. Some of the residents even still played the piano and were always and enthusiastically encouraged to do so.

Pastor David Cameron did not play the piano, and when as a working minister he did try and sing, it was passion rather than a strict adherence to the melody that drove him on. Music was background. Pleasant ,of course, but no help now. He was, here in this shapeless and dehumanized situation, a sorry shadow of his former self. He loathed his shriveled, useless body and lacked the chemicals and the muscular coordination to put an end to it. While he was a physical prisoner to the ravages of the stroke, his still sharp mind and restless curiosity struggled against and within the confines of his slackened body. He often broke into a tear-streaked sweat trying to say those few garbled words that remained to him, trying to give voice to the intelligent, crystal clear thoughts that were still there and permanently trapped inside his head.

Months of intense and often frustrating physical

therapy had enabled him to use three fingers on his right hand well enough to operate his oversized tablet. This impersonal device was his lifeline to cogent thinking, to the world of ideas, to news of the outside world, to theological research and discourse and eventually, the possibility of going back to writing the book he'd started so many years ago.

He was not a happy or a contented man, but he was still alive, and he was still resourceful. He could do nothing to change the length of his remaining days on earth; nature would eventually take care of that. What he could do was practice what he used to preach: "Make the most of each and every day in your own way, and let God take care of the rest." Even if he had long since discarded the God part of the axiom, he himself could make the most what he had left. The truth was, he had no choice. Where there was a will would be a way, and David Edward Cameron would make damn sure he'd find it.

CHAPTER 15

Frederick and Olympia were both dozing lightly when Jim and Andrew pulled into the drive and parked behind the big blue van. Olympia pushed at her hair, hoping she didn't look too disheveled, and then autocorrected. What's the problem? This was her friend Jim. He was a total fusspot about his own appearance, but he would never question hers.

The two men got out of the car, Andrew in white shorts and a Hawaiian shirt, and Jim in pale blue shorts and a lighter blue shirt. Olympia realized with a silent giggle that she'd never seen Jim's legs before this day and credited Andrew with the slow unbuttoning of her best friend.

"Looking good," she yelled in greeting, and not bothering with any further preliminaries added, "What did you bring for dinner?"

Olympia was Jim's favorite food fan. As much as she

enjoyed cooking herself, Jim had raised it to the level of an art. She could only imagine how good this was going to be.

"Actually, I brought Chinese." Jim was trying to stifle a smile.

"Listen to him," countered Andrew, brushing away the thought. "He'd no more bring Chinese than he'd bring fish fingers to the queen's tea. You just wait. Besides, I'm the only queen around here, and I tell you, I didn't order it."

Jim rolled his eyes. He never indulged in gay jokes or flashy behavior. Andrew, however, made the most of a good thing. Olympia thought Jim's reticence might have been a result of the years of hiding that he had suffered or the natural conservative nature of the man, but either way, it mattered not. Jim was conservative in dress and nature, and Andrew was a jazz pianist and a sometimes naughty breath of love and fresh air. They met in mid-life, and both bore the scars of growing up gay in a time when coming out could be life threatening. They still chose their friends carefully.

"How about we go inside and put things away?" Frederick stood and bowed and gestured toward the kitchen door. "After you, gentlemen, and you too, good lady wife."

Olympia gathered up the tea glasses and Frederick's crossword and took up the rear.

Inside, Jim explained in mouthwatering detail what that night's repast would be. He loved doing this, and for him it was as much a part of the event as the food itself.

Gastronomical foreplay perhaps? Or perhaps an orchestral overture or prologue. Choose your metaphor, Olympia, Jim is on a roll.

He told them they would start with a cold cucumber soup, which would be followed by a full Salade Nicoise for the men, and the same elegant assemblage without the imported Italian tuna for vegetarian Olympia. It was a summer favorite, a salad that was in and of itself a fully balanced meal. Potatoes, tomatoes, sliced hard boiled eggs, lettuce, fresh shallots and the tuna, all tossed in a delicately herbed vinaigrette.

All this would be served with the fresh bread they'd picked up in a favorite bakery in Boston's North End. Afterwards, for the crowning glory, they would finish with one of Andrew's specialties, a summer fruits Pavlova topped with fresh whipped cream.

OMG, thought Olympia, remembering the hard cheese in the fridge and the soft crackers in the pantry, what in hell can I set out for hors d'oeuvres? She remembered her mother calling them "horse's ovaries," and the thought never failed to bring a smile to her face. But it was Frederick who came to the rescue.

"When you told me you were coming, I took it upon myself to get a little something to go with the pre-dinner wine, and I think I may have hit it just right."

Olympia felt a sense of cold dread creeping up her spine. Frederick alone in a supermarket was always an adventure. She fully expected a plate of popcorn and fried pickles

"Voila!" He pulled a pizza shaped box out of the

fridge, pulled it open and held it out for all to see and admire.

So much for presentation, thought Olympia, steeling herself for the worst.

"Here we have, gentlemen and good wife, a selection of olives, some mini-vegetarian sushi, a bowl of tamarind almonds and a horseradish cheese spread with assorted rice crackers."

Olympia could not believe her ears or her eyes. "Frederick ... how did you ... it's perfect."

"I asked for assistance," Frederick touched the side of his nose with the tip of his index finger. "Believe it or not, there are some things you are not privy to. When Jim told me what he was going to make, I took myself to the high class supermarket, the new one across town, and asked the woman at the deli counter what I should get. She put it all together for me." Frederick was beaming like a kid who had just put away his training wheels.

"Well done you." Olympia was unexpedtedly full of pride for the dear man she'd met in the Maine woods all those years ago.

Frederick favored them all with a sweeping bow of acknowledgment and began setting out the delicacies.

"Let me set the table, and you can pour the wine, Jim. You know where we keep the glasses. Why don't we have our pre-dinner delights out in the screen room? The light is absolutely lovely at this time of day. No humidity and a light breeze. It'll be perfect."

Olympia knew they wouldn't get down to the serious part of the conversation until after dinner and over thimblefuls of ancient French brandy. She also knew that the two men would likely stay the night so they could fully enjoy the wines that Jim would have meticulously selected to go with each and every segment of the meal, but meanwhile, she could address the lesser of the two issues confronting her and her new ministry, the lady and the dog.

"Does anyone mind if Jim and I engage in a little shop talk before dinner?

"How little is little?" asked Frederick.

"On a scale of one to ten, with a misconducting minister at fifteen, I'd say this is a three or a four and maybe even a zero."

Jim picked up the thread. "Earlier today you told me about me a woman who came to church with her service dog. You told me she seemed kind of needy, which you'd more or less expect if she required a comfort dog. She goes to coffee hour, stays on to help clean up and then aggravates the matriarchs because she wants water for the dog on their clean floor."

"In between the coffee hour clean-up and the dog water, she came back into the study to see me and hinted at, but wouldn't really elucidate on, what the nature of her problems might be. She said she was getting over chemo for breast cancer, hence the hat and dark glasses. She told me that she still couldn't work but was hoping to get back soon. She made a number of vaguely ambiguous personal statements, you know, the kind that invite clarification? Then, when I did ask, she'd pivot away and change the subject. It's a familiar getting you to know me game. It took a while, but eventually we talked about dogs and cars, about as neutral as you can get.

Finally, she told me she'd like to come back, and then added the pity-me clause 'if you really want me to.'"

"In other words convince me, beg me even, and then I might favor you with a return visit." Jim raised his wine-glass. "You've got this one, reverend lady. Cheers!"

"Amen to that, and let's eat!" Olympia led the charge.

CHAPTER 16

J im's dinner and Andrew's Pavlova exceeded all
expectations, and now the four of them were
sprawled in cushioned bamboo easy chairs
watching fireflies flickering in the last light of a
summer evening outside the conservatory. Frederick's
Conservatory. Some would call it a sun room. It was the
latest testament to his often circuitous and sometimes
hazardous-to-his-own-health interest in home improvement projects.

While they were chatting and taking mini-sips of
their ancient and honorable brandy, the two cats circled
around their legs and feet, selecting which lap they would
grace with their purring presence. Olympia took the next
few minutes to explain in greater detail what she had
uncovered in the pastor's study, what the church administrator did and didn't say, and her own thoughts about
how it all may have transpired.

"It seems a shame to wreck such a beautiful meal and

gastronomical afterglow with what is a really disgusting change of subject, but …"

"That's one of the reasons we came down, my friend. Clergy sex abuse is bad stuff. As a former Catholic priest, I can attest to the damage that this kind of crime and its cover-up can cause to the individual victim or victims involved, as well as the whole fabric of trust within a church community. It's the monster under the bed that no one will talk about, but they all keep feeding it so they can keep it alive."

Olympia nodded wordlessly.

"And you say this guy is totally out of the picture now?"

"Work-wise, he is. He had a massive stroke in April. From what I understand, he can't walk or use his left side at all and very little of his right, so he needs to be fed and his other bodily needs attended to by a caregiver. He can hear, but he can barely talk. According to the Church Administrator who told me all of this at lunch today, he's still compos mentis, he just can't get the words out. I suppose that's the real tragedy. He understands every-thing, even reads books on the computer with his one good eye, but he's in diapers and needs twenty-four-hour care, and the family can't manage him on their own."

"You could say he's created his own living hell and leave him to it," said Frederick. "He's never going to go after anyone again."

"That's not the point," Jim leaned forward. "Not to make a joke of it, but sexual abuse is the gift that keeps on giving. The damage goes on for years and even into the next generation unless the victims are at least given the opportunity to bear safe witness to what happened to them and be believed. And that's just the individual victims. The congregation is also a victim. They are a living testament to the tangled web of lies and shame. The persistent denial. The explicit or implicit cooperation on the part of some of the members who looked the other way, people who knew exactly what was going on but didn't want to bring scandal down on the community."

"I guess I didn't think about all of the other implications." He rubbed his chin with one hand and absently stroked the sleek black cat with the other. "Growing up in England, we lived by the axiom, 'least said, soonest mended.' We simply didn't talk about unpleasant things on the theory that if you didn't talk about them, you wouldn't think about them, and if you didn't even think about them, they would go away."

"Only they don't." Andrew, who until then had been a silent observer and the landing pad for the other cat, added, "When you bury pain and shame, it only gets worse, and it can mess up everything you do. Trust me," he whispered, "I know."

Jim reached out for Andrew's hand and blessed him with a gentle smile.

After a quiet moment Olympia asked, "So what do I do, Jim? I am way out of my comfort zone, and much as I'd like to run in the opposite direction, we all know I'm not going to walk away from this. I need advice."

Jim thought for a few minutes. "I'll ask my buddy over at the Dorchester Police Headquarters to run a criminal background search on Cameron and see if anything comes up. Any past allegations or inquiries of a compromising nature? The problem is that because it's an independent, unaffiliated community church, there will be no hierarchical record keeping, open or closed, like there would be in larger, more interconnected denominational churches. The only place you are likely to find anything might be in the meeting notes of old board or vestry meetings, but to be honest, this kind of thing doesn't usually make it into the public record."

"What about the newspapers?" asked Frederick.

Jim shook his head. "Only if there was a public scandal. If something like this does make into the media, then it's out there for all to see, and the guy—and it usually is a man—is out of there on the next bus. No, from what you say, I think this thing was ongoing for some time and from then until now has been deeply buried. I also think more people know about it than anyone is saying. It's probably been conspiracy of silence for years…and they're all victims."

"Damn," said Olympia.

"That's one way of putting it," said Jim, "but if you want my advice, I would say what I always say when you find a wrong you need to right. Ask questions discreetly, take copious notes, and talk to people in the town who are not members of the church. Meanwhile, distressing as it sounds, see if you can recognize any of the faces of the victims from the pictures."

Olympia grimaced in disgust.

"Put a piece of paper over the explicit stuff, and simply frame out the face. I'll show you how to do it.

That's step one. Then take a close-up of the face with your phone, and then do a Google face or image search."

She looked horrified. "Are you kidding? I don't want to have my name associated with any of this. You know what happens if you click on a porn site by accident. Or maybe you're writing a sermon, and you look into something unsavory as part of the research, and you get stalked for weeks with targeted ads."

"Olympia, people these days create alternative identities using different names and a Yahoo addresses for just this very thing, remaining anonymous. You haven't read enough mystery and crime novels, my dear. You might consider it, and I can even recommend a few." He winked.

"Who knew." Olympia wasted no time and was already thinking about what to name her new imaginary friend when her cell phone rang and the beehive clock in the sitting room *boinged* loudly enough to startle them all.

"Uh oh," said Frederick. "Somebody's not happy in there."

Olympia grabbed her phone and went outside into the back yard to take the call.

Andrew pointed to the interior of the house with a mystified expression on his face. "Who were you referring to? Is there someone else in the house?"

Jim laughed. "Do you want to tell him the story, Frederick, or shall I? I do know it word for word."

"Of course you do. You are rather part of the family, old boy, and it is part of the family history. I'm not at all sure we didn't tell it at Christmas, but with all the noise and happy confusion, I can't remember. Why don't you do the honors this time, Jim, and I'll keep notes and make the necessary corrections should you stray too far from the proven record."

By now, Andrew was completely confused, and the other two men were playing off each other and stretching out the game for as long as they could. Then Jim cleared his throat and called for attention.

"I'll do him a mercy and give him the short version. Once upon a time …"

"Oh for God's sake, mon, get on with it."

Jim giggled and settled into the story. "Once upon a time, right after Frederick and Olympia bought this house, they found an old diary and a beehive clock in a secret cupboard. Both items belonged to the last titled owner, because the diary describes the clock, and we know the author of the diary was the last living descendant of Otis Winslow the man who built the house. Olympia has the diary, but she and Frederick have joint custody of the clock—or maybe it's the other way around. It's possible the clock keeps custody of them."

"So far I am not enlightened," said Andrew.

"Hang in there, my love. I'm getting there. The clock does not keep time, but it does make its presence known on a regular basis. We think the clock has a connection to the last owner, Leanna Faith Winslow—author of the diary, Mayflower descendent and resident house ghost. It appears that even after she died, the old girl never left the place, and when she senses danger she warns us through the clock."

Andrew made a face. He was clearly not believing a word of it.

"No, really," said Jim. "I didn't believe it when I first heard it, but the lady knows her business."

"And all of ours, as well," added Frederick. "She is a noisy and a nosey little so-and-so, but we've come to love her."

"And clearly there's something on her mind tonight."

Frederick nodded in agreement. "It's most likely related to whatever is happening at Olympia's church. The woman sees trouble before we do. I just wish she could talk so she could tell us what it is."

"If you don't mind, I'll adopt the wait-and-see approach to all of this," said Andrew.

"Well, if I know Miss Winslow, you won't have to wait too long."

"Wait too long for what," asked Olympia, letting the outside door fall shut behind her.

"The clock's been making a bit of a ruckus in there. There's trouble brewing somewhere. Who was it that called, my love?"

Olympia did a little twirl in the middle of the room. "It seems like the ladies of the church are planning a welcome luncheon and asked me when I might be available?"

"Did you remind them that you are on your summer schedule, and you only go in one day a week?"

"I did, and they asked if I would make an exception and come in this Saturday. I don't mind. I'd rather do a little extra time in the beginning and get the lay of the land on a more relaxed schedule. That way, I won't be in for so many surprises when we start up in the fall."

"Thus spake Zarathustra."

"Wise-ass," said his wife.

Jim chuckled at their erudite repartee and began clearing off the coffee table when Andrew called out from the sitting room.

"Did one of you start a fire in the woodstove? It's the middle of summer!"

"We didn't," said Frederick, "but I jolly well know who did. She's deadly serious, Olympia. You may have a bigger problem on your hands than you think you do."

"Wonderful," said Olympia. "Just want I always wanted. Something to do in my spare time—putting out fires."

CHAPTER 17

Most evenings after they'd had their dinner, Rayna and her mother would watch TV for an hour or so, usually the news and maybe a game show, if the old woman stayed awake long enough. When her eyelids began to droop, and she started nodding off, Rayna would help her get washed up and into her nightgown and then help her into bed. The woman could still do most of these things for herself, and she did, but Rayna preferred to be within earshot in case she needed help. Independence was important, but when you are of a certain age, unexpected things can happen. Rayna had a love-hate relationship with her mother, but her mother would only ever know about the love part.

When she was safely tucked in, a glass of water on the night stand and the nightlight switched on in the corner by the door, Rayna wished her mother good night and whistled for Raggsy. In an instant the animal, who was sitting outside the door, was at her side, and the two of them went up the stairs to the second floor and settled into her private workroom. Night after night she worked on her precious scrapbooks, sorting, cutting, pasting and retrieving news clippings from her files and all the while, under her breath, whistling the play-party songs she had sung as a child: "Farmer in the Dell," "Jack and Jill" and "Wee Willie Winkie."

Rayna was particularly eager to get upstairs and get started tonight. She was in her happy place and starting work on a brand new scrapbook. While she usually had a general idea of how she would design them, she also knew that her projects sometimes had minds of their own.

AFTER OLYMPIA AGREED TO COME TO LUNCH AND MEET the board on the following Saturday, the Fosselberg twins were on the phone for the rest of the evening. Within two hours they had commandeered several volunteers to bake up some of their finest creations and, more importantly, to come in the day before and dust and clean and polish the church parlor within an inch of its hundred-and-fifty-year life. The South River Community Church was going to look and smell better than it had in years.

The twins were well aware that their numbers had been dwindling and that the yearly pledges were at an all-time low. One or the other of them had sat on the board for over thirty years and counting. They would certainly miss the comfort and continuity that they'd had with Pastor Dave, but not a one of them could have prevented what happened, and they had no choice but to move on. And although neither of them would admit it, a breath of fresh air might be just what the congregation needed. Was it a blessing in disguise or could it be a double-edged sword?

"A new broom sweeps clean," they told each other over and over again, words their mother had often said to them. "But an old broom gets in all the corners," was what their grandmother used to say under her breath in response.

Reverend Doctor Olympia Brown was certainly a new broom, but did they still have need of an old one? Each twin had asked this privately of herself. Perhaps it would be in everyone's interest simply to avoid those nasty old dusty corners, let sleeping dogs lie and move on.

CHAPTER 18

As was often the case, Jim and Andrew spent the night and the next morning stayed on for a few hours in order to avoid the sluggish Boston commuter traffic. After a late and relaxed breakfast out in the sunny conservatory, Jim and Olympia went into Olympia's office. The plan was to see if there was a way they could produce viable and useable facial images from the lurid and incriminating photographs in Pastor Dave's secret files. Frederick, who was having none of this, was in a much lighter frame of mind and invited Andrew to join him in a stroll around the back garden. When they were well out of earshot, he quietly outlined the secret plans for his once and future water garden.

In the privacy of her home office, Olympia opened the folder containing the photographs and spread them out across her desk. Jim blew out a long breath and Olympia chewed on her lower lip as they two looked down at the incredibly sad and disturbing display.

"This is awful," whispered Olympia. "How in God's name did he get away with it for so long? Those poor women. Part of me wants to weep, and part of me wants to throw up. How did he do it for so long?"

"You've partially answered your own question," said Jim. "As a former Catholic, I can tell you what I learned about cover-up and complicity. It's fear and shame coupled with institutionally complicit denial and cover-up and a fuckingly hideous abuse of the power of the position. If victims did get the courage to say something, who would believe them? No one could ever speak badly of the parish priest. It simply wasn't allowed. His word was God, and the abusers knew it. From what little you've told me, the guy was a charmer. His wife took the kids and left him. That alone speaks volumes. He never remarried?"

Jim was not a man given to swearing, and when he did, it was in times of helpless outrage.

"That must have been awful. What did you do when the whole abuse thing in the Catholic church blew up?"

"I never told anyone, not even you, Olympia. But when the sex abuse scandal was reported in the *Boston Globe* in 2004, and all hell broke loose, my DPD buddy called me in on the QT to see if I could give them any information. I could, and I did, and it broke my heart. Blurry facial recognition and computer enhancement was part of the process even back then. I identified men, priests, my long-time colleagues, as the abusers who would eventually be exposed, defrocked and ultimately excommunicated. What they did broke my trust, and what I did to identify them and why I had no choice but to do it broke my heart. It was like I was two people: Father Jim, the parish priest at St. Brendan's, and Jim Sawicki, the kid from the west end of Boston helping out his Irish Catholic childhood bestie behind the scenes. You know, Jim the rat."

"I'm surprised you stayed on in the church as long as you did. I wish you could have told me."

"Even if I had, what could I do? Where could I go? I'm a priest. Even if I was betrayed by the institution that ordained me, I still felt called and committed to the service of God. Remember when I went away on that retreat in Kentucky all those years ago? Well, that was part of it. I needed to get clean myself. I felt stained by it all."

"Oh, Jim." Olympia reached for his hand and held it for a long moment. "That must have been so hard for you."

"You have no idea."

"No, I think maybe I do." She squeezed his hand again and released it. "Okay, my friend, let's do this."

In less time than they might have imagined, they found five images they felt they could work with. So as not to disturb the surface of the originals, they framed out just the faces with strips of paper and photographed them.

Then, after a quick coffee break, Olympia watched over Jim's shoulder as he meticulously brought each face into clearer and more painful focus.

"Now what do we do?" asked Olympia.

"I'm going to take one set of the facial images over to my friend at police headquarters and use their advanced technology to do an image search. I suggest you start by memorizing the faces and taking a good look at the women in your new congregation to see if you recognize any of them."

"Good God, Jim, you don't think any of them would still be there after something like that? I would never want to look at the guy again."

"Abuse and victimhood is a study in itself, and it's way beyond me. Just ask yourself how many women you know who stay in abusive relationships, and when the first one dissolves, they go find themselves another one. Humans are dark and complex creatures, Olympia. Maybe that's why you and I do what we do. Remember the words of the prophet Isaiah: 9:2 'The people that walked in darkness have seen a great light: they that dwell in the land of the shadow of death, upon them hath the light shined.' We are trying to bring in the light, Reverend Doctor girlfriend, each of us in our own way."

Not that she needed reminding, but in that moment, standing next to him, she remembered all of the reasons why she loved this man and why their bond was so very deep.

LATER THAT AFTERNOON AFTER LUNCH, WITH JIM AND Andrew well on their way back into Boston, Olympia was feeling agitated and restless. When Frederick offered to make them some tea, she declined and told him she needed to go for a walk.

"Shall I come with you?" he asked.

She shook her head. "Nothing personal, my love. I need some think time."

"It's about the pictures, isn't it?"

"Right in one. I'm going to go for a walk on the beach. Maybe I'll get lucky and find some sea glass while I'm at it. I won't be gone all that long."

"Keep your phone with you."

"And you remember to keep yours on."

"Don't forget the sunscreen."

"I love you, Frederick. You can chill some wine while I'm out."

THE NEARBY DUXBURY BEACH WAS ALMOST EMPTY. The swimmers and the sunbathers and the families with their children had gone home to start supper. All that remained were a few beachcombers, dog walkers with their plastic bags, a single fisherman and a couple of other solitary walkers like herself taking in the low light of the afternoon and the soft sounds of the waves nibbling at the sand pebbles.

Olympia was of an age when walking barefoot on the sand and stones was not a good idea. She had, therefore, put on a pair of ratty beach-sneakers she kept in the van for the purpose and was now sloshing along, ankle deep in seawater at the water's undulating edge and wrestling with her opposing angels.

One of the inner voices told her this was way-way-way beyond her skill set, that it would be best for all concerned if she simply presented the awful evidence to the board/vestry, gave them a list of consulting organizations that worked with churches facing these issues, declined their invitation to be their pastor, and left them to handle it.

The counter argument was that in these situations, it was likely that more than a few people already knew what was going on and wanted to keep the whole matter swept under the rug in the pastor's study, where it would stay, continuing to fester and poison the very air they breathed. Was it her job to make them face it? Did she really want to take something like this on? Maybe this was work for a younger minister and not a grandmother.

The other voices simply kept chanting, "If not you, then who," and after multiple repetitions, the doers won the argument.

"I'm getting too old for this, dammit," she yelled into the waves.

This time, the arguing angels remained silent, and the Reverend Doctor Olympia Brown had the beginnings of a plan.

WHEN SHE GOT BACK HOME, FREDERICK HAD A GLASS of wine, covered with plastic wrap, waiting in the fridge. After years of being married to this curious, passionate woman, he knew what the outcome of her alone time would be. He also knew that she would need him to hear her out and thereby clarify it in her own mind before she could move on. It was part of her process, and he absolutely adored and respected it and secretly thanked his lucky stars that he could be an integral part of it. When Frederick introduced himself as "the minister's wife," as he often did, it wasn't simply a humorous, Frederick-y quip. Frederick was the real thing.

CHAPTER 19

Olympia hadn't planned to go back to the church until the luncheon on Saturday, but after having talked the whole thing over with Jim and her walk on the beach with her competing angels, she revised her plan. Tomorrow she would make what Frederick would call "a hit and run raid" to the church. Go, get in and get back out as fast as she could with no witnesses.

The thought had occurred to her that there might be some old church membership photo directories stashed in the office somewhere. These would have pictures of past members of the congregation when they were younger than they were now and it was possible she might find a match there. If no one at all expected that she would be in, and Becci, bless her, wasn't there to ask questions, she could go through the place with a fine-toothed comb and see what else the unsavory pastor might have left in his wake.

The grim reality hit her like a sledgehammer. If she did find a match, what then? How do you start a bonfire that could very well cost you your job, not to mention turn someone else's world upside down? She didn't have an answer for that yet, but Jim was her go-to person. She'd be counting on him every step of the way through this. Whatever the case, she knew it was going to be an uneasy week unless she could find something to do that would move things forward. Waiting was not one of her strong points. If she didn't do something, she knew she would spend the rest of the week in agitated thumb twiddling.

Then it came to her. She was the new pastor, and what do all new pastors do? They make home visits so they can get to know the members of the congregation individually and vice versa. They look up the names and addresses of former members and invite them to come back. It was snooping in plain sight and getting paid for it, as well. Where do you find those names and addresses? In the pastor's study, of course. And because you are so very thoughtful and considerate, you don't bother the church administrator when she is having time off. Of course you don't. Olympia liked having this kind of conversation with herself.

CHAPTER 20

On Thursday morning Olympia chose to make an exception to her practice of not working alone in an empty church. By now she was certain there was more to be found in that musty office and elsewhere, for that matter. She also feared that if anyone at all got wind of what she was doing, they might try to stop her. Thus, time was of the essence.

Shortly after breakfast she told Frederick what she was up to, approximately when she thought she'd be home, air-kissed him good-bye and headed for her van. In truth, she was looking forward to the drive and the time alone. As she so often did, she used time alone in the car, and sometimes walking on beaches, to clear her head and focus her thinking.

She knew full well that looking through forgotten boxes in dusty attics and digging around in the cluttered corners of unused closets was best done solo. The last thing she wanted to do at this stage of the inquiry, and it was an inquiry, was to give anyone—Becci, for example —the slightest inkling of what she was up to. She wanted no questions about why she was digging around in the murky recesses of church history. If anyone did come in while she was there, she would simply say she was working on clearing up the office, and she didn't want to bother anyone, which of course was absolutely true.

She would not go on to say she was doing it with the intention of muddying up some pretty stagnant water.

If she and/or Jim managed to find a clear match, and that victim was willing to come forward, all hell would break loose. On the other hand, if, despite their combined efforts along with those of the Dorchester and Boston police departments, they could not find a match, then what? Should she simply drop it, or should she take the disgusting evidence to the board and let them deal with it? She didn't feel she could take the pictures to the police without permission from the victims. After that only the victims themselves could legally press charges, and that would be an entirely different undertaking.

Whatever the outcome, there was no doubt in her mind that she was about to open a really vile can of worms, and despite the potential for consummate ugliness, she saw no way out. The only way was forward and through and see it to the end. She'd made a personal commitment to those haunting faces in the blurry lurid photographs, and in moments of doubt or asking herself why she felt so compelled to act, she reminded herself once again of other victims she'd known and helped. They were the reason.

Crimes of sexual abuse and molestation are crimes of

the worst kind. Most are committed in secret and then hidden away to fester and putrefy and stink and poison anything that comes in contact with it/them for years if not generations to come. Olympia also knew that her diligence would most likely be neither welcome nor rewarded by a power group somewhere within a church that had tacitly enabled this behavior for years. The question is always, why?

The most frequent answers are usually fear of scandal, fear of exposure, tacit admission of secret complicit behavior, and fear of change, as in the devil we know and have some control over is better than someone new that we will have to bend to our ways, a classic bargain with the devil.

Olympia knew all too well that sexual misconduct was and is no stranger to churches or, for that matter, any other institution where most of the power is vested in the hands of one person. Maybe it is because churches are outwardly committed to more lofty ideals and their members holding themselves to a higher moral standard that the crime seems so particularly heinous. The righteous indignation the perpetrators throw up in defense of themselves is twice as revolting, because it is so very hypocritical.

Olympia was working herself into a full-scaled rant. She could do that. The subject made her blood boil. No, these good people, and she really did believe that most members of the congregation were good people, were hiding a community secret, and it was the three deadly sisters of fear, guilt and shame that were keeping them all from speaking.

When she pulled up and parked in the empty church lot, she knew none of this would be in the letter of agreement they had yet to write up. She also knew, as she unlocked and pushed open the side door and then clicked it securely shut behind her, the day would come when she would likely be viciously challenged, if not outright accused of purposeful slander and malicious, libelous action for doing this.

Her footsteps sounded unnaturally loud in a building that was empty and uncomfortably warm and airless. Even the dust motes visible in the shafts of light coming through the windows in the corridor looked hot and stale. Only the sure knowledge that there was an air conditioner in the study and a couple of floor fans ready for action kept her moving forward.

After plugging in and activating the fans and the air-conditioner, Olympia swallowed half a bottle of water and set to work. The most obvious place for old church publications to be kept would be in a file somewhere, and since files are usually kept in file cabinets, the file cabinet on the wall behind the pastor's desk was her first stop. She noted that she still thought of the desk in the study to be "the pastor's desk" and not yet her desk. And then, remembering what she'd found there, she knew why. Would it ever feel like her own desk, she wondered, running her hands over the beautiful wood in front of her? Did she want it to feel like her desk? Considering its lurid history, probably not.

Olympia found what she was looking for in less than twenty minutes, just as the fans and the air-conditioned ground to a simultaneous halt. Crap! She tried turning on the overhead light. Nothing. Double-crap! She'd likely overloaded the circuit and blown a fuse. Not surprising in a building as old as this and in need of so much upgrading and repair, but still, not a little embarrassing. She'd leave a note in the buildings and grounds mail box and send an email to Becci and apologize profusely, but she still had work to do, and the temperature in the room full of secrets was rising rapidly.

In a wooden file cabinet directly behind her desk she found what she needed, a collection of old church picture directories with names, addresses and even a few email addresses. In addition to this there were old parish record books containing listings and even some photographs of the weddings, christenings and funerals celebrated at South River Community Church.

The oldest one went all the way back to the year the church was established, 1860. The more recent ones recorded the dates of services and celebrations officiated by Pastor David. E. Cameron. Would they have the faces, and by default the names and addresses, she was looking for? At the very least it was a place to start.

She pulled the whole lot out and dumped it on the desk for sorting, then almost jumped out of her skin when the office phone rang. She automatically started to reach for the phone when her innate good sense reminded her that offices had answering machines for a reason. She would listen to the message and if she felt it needed immediate attention, she would pick up.

The call was routine, someone asking for the time of the Sunday service, and if they offered child care. Becci would take care of that when she called in for the messages. But the interruption served another more focused and more prudent purpose. Olympia really didn't want to be caught out at what she was doing. She gave thought to the very real possibility that anyone could drop in unannounced like Rayna had done the other day. Her unmistakable vehicle was out there in the parking lot for all to see, and she was here with both hands, metaphorically speaking, of course, in the cookie jar.

Considering that she'd already found quite a bit to work with right in the office, and the probable life-threatening heat she would encounter in the windowless attic, Olympia made a quick change of plans. She would leave the attic for another day and work at home after all. She collected the membership books covering the years of Pastor Dave's tenure as an added source of addresses and telephone numbers, should she need them, and the red leather-bound Parish Records. She slipped all of this into her tote bag and draped one of her flowing silk scarves over the lot of it as camouflage.

She had a printer at home that could make copies, if needed, and her own desk in her own office was one hell of a lot safer, cooler and more private place to work than was this roomful of dusty lies and hidden secrets.

She checked her watch. She could be home in time for lunch and have the rest of the afternoon to work on all of this. She hiked her tote bag, quite heavy now, over her left shoulder and started down the corridor. She was almost to the door when it opened, seemingly by itself, and scared the bejesus out of her.

"Pastor! What an unexpected treat." It was the

Fosselbergs, both fully turned out in their summer gardening attire: grand garden hats, multi-pocketed bib aprons, kneeling pads and plastic watering cans. They were armed and ready for action.

"We didn't expect to find you here. Are you coming or going? We just came by to water the flowers and get things started for our luncheon on Saturday. We have planned a totally vegetarian meal in your honor. Do you have time for a cup of tea?"

"Actually, I just came by to get some things I needed that I left in the file cabinet. After next week I'd like to start making some home visits to members of the congregation, and to do that, I'll need a parish directory. I'd love to stay and help you with the garden, but word has it that Frederick—that's my husband, and I'm sure you'll meet him soon—is making lunch. It's an offer I dare not refuse."

She winked broadly at the two smiling ladies and walked as quickly as she could right past them and out into the parking lot, saying nothing about the blown fuse. Since they would be working outside, it really didn't make any sense. Why bother them?

She had told them truth. She *was* going off to have lunch with Frederick, and she did need a church directory, and it was not a lie not to say how many she needed. As far as the pastoral records went, they would be coming back along with everything else on Saturday morning. Olympia did not like to lie and never did unless she absolutely had to. But in her way of thinking, delicately evading full disclosure was perfectly acceptable. Her mother called it, "an error of omission."

CHAPTER 21

O nce in the car, safely buckled in with the air conditioning on high and the radio blasting a double violin concerto by J.S. Bach, she went back into her planning/problem solving/driving mode. She was thinking about the very real possibility of finding a match—and then what? You don't just walk up to that person and tell her you found the most awful picture of her. She parked that thought in the 'Things-to-Ask-Jim basket' and went into her thinking zone.

She would start by making routine calls to fallen away or non-attending members, introducing herself as the new pastor at South River and asking if they'd like her to come by and pay them a visit.

And what if one of the women you call is a match? Do you bring up the subject of the former minister and ask what he was like, or do you just treat it as a normal visit and let her take the lead? What if you have a perfect match, and the perfect match tells you to get out and never darken her door again? You do as you are asked, and get out. On the way home you say a prayer for guidance, and you keep on digging until you find someone who will speak up, because if you don't, the church and the congregation will never be healthy, and the whole ugly thing could play out again. Olympia knew that over a dozen women whose lives had been shattered by one man's hypocritical lust and greed were out there hiding in the shadows. Olympia realized that there were women she was about to meet who may or may not thank her for finding them.

And, she added in a disillusioned afterthought to self, none of this is news, and it will happen again … and again … until the victims take back their power.

TWO HOURS LATER SHE WAS BACK IN HER HOME OFFICE, a workspace Frederick had created for her by repurposing a cold storage pantry. She sat down at her desk and pulled the most current church directory out of her tote bag. Already two years out of date, the directory showed a total count of sixty-three adults plus seven kids who were not old enough to be voting members. She even recognized a few faces from that past Sunday but none from the photographs in the bottom drawer.

Last Sunday there were thirty-five in church…not a bad percentage. They were probably just curious about me, she thought, and wondered what the attendance might be on the coming Sunday, then reminded herself that summer attendance in any church was minimal at best. Year-round pastors often saved their best sermons for the academic year, and in the summer months they either recycled old sermons or relied on congregational participation in a more relaxed atmosphere and format.

Being new, and following a ministry and a minister surrounded by dark secrets that ended abruptly with the man being carried out of the church on a stretcher, Olympia did not have that option. She had hard work to do right now. These poor people were still in shock. For more reasons than she ever could have anticipated, she had to be on her toes, every single one of them, starting on day one. Stop ruminating, woman, and get on with the task at hand, she told herself.

She opened the colorful, spiral-bound directory, noted a few familiar faces, the same ones as on Sunday, and was about to power up her cell phone when the house phone rang. It was Rayna.

"Oh, hi, Pastor. I hope I'm not bothering you, but do you have a few minutes?"

There was only one response, and she delivered it through clenched teeth. "Of course, Rayna, but only a few. I have to make a phone call in a few minutes." This, of course was partially true, and it set a limit.

"Oh, I can call back later." Olympia could just see the apologetic woman cringing and wringing her hands, and then she stopped herself lest a snarky little thought came through in the tone of her voice.

"No no, I'm here. How can I help you?"

"It's about next Sunday. Do you think I could bring some flowers for the altar or maybe some cookies for coffee hour? If I'm going to be there anyway, I might as well contribute something, don't you think?"

"I think that's a lovely idea, Rayna. Cookies, I think.

Thelma and Selma Fosselberg told me they do the flowers in the summer. I guess they have a show-stopper of a garden, and they love to share the bounty."

"So I shouldn't bring flowers, because they wouldn't be wanted."

By now, if Olympia could have gotten her hands on the woman's shoulders, she would have given her a really good shake. She loathed this kind of self-effacing manipulation which Rayna Buxton seemed to have raised to fine art.

She spoke slowly, declaratively and painstakingly explicitly. "No, Rayna, what I said was, cookies would be lovely and most welcome. There can never be enough cookies, don't you think? At least not in my opinion. I'm a cookie addict, but don't ever tell anyone, okay? The Fosselberg ladies love to do the flowers. They've done the summer flowers forever, I think. It's one of those church tradition things, and the last thing a new minister does is go anywhere near church traditions. Do, however, please bring some cookies on Sunday and I'll see that you get a chance to bring some flowers later on."

"Okay." She sounded mollified and then asked, "What's your favorite cookie?"

Olympia wanted to scream, Oreos, dammit woman, mint Oreos, in a family-sized package. You get them at the goddamned supermarket, and don't bother me! But she restrained herself.

"Anything with oatmeal and molasses or with ginger and sometimes chocolate chips. In other words, I like all kinds. Surprise me."

"That sounds like a fun idea. I'll do that. Thank you, Pastor."

"See you on Sunday."

Only after she disconnected the call did she realize she had not given her home phone number to anyone at the church. On the other hand, even though cell phones were taking over the world and paper phone directories, thick enough for a child or a short adult to sit on, were ancient history, directory assistance was still available to the curious and the persistent.

She sat, drumming her fingers on the desk. The day was getting on, and so far she'd made no progress. Even though she had a home office and a door she could shut, on some days there were far too many distractions for her to be able to concentrate, and now she was hungry.

According to the note Frederick left on the kitchen table, he'd gone back to the home and garden store to make some alterations in the recently disputed land and waterscape plans. This mean the man could come home in the next ten minutes or at dinner time.

Olympia went back into the kitchen where the cats began twirling figure eights around her ankles and carrying on as if they hadn't eaten in days. "One of these days I'm going to trip over you two and break a leg, and will you care? No-o-o-o! It's all about the food, isn't it? Frederick calls it 'cupboard love,' and he's right. Come on then."

She pulled a handful of treats out of the bag on the shelf, fired them across the room and giggled as Cadeau and Thunderfoot charged after them. Now she could make it to the fridge without incident, and there she pulled out the makings of a quick but sustaining lunch. A generous scoop of egg salad, something green to keep it company on the plate and a tomato she would slice to complete the picture of health and well-being. The deep dive into the cookies would come later.

She carried the food back to her office, spread it out on the work table beside the desk and set to work. Within fifteen minutes of uploading the first tortured image into the search box she had a match. Olympia didn't know whether to shout hallelujah or burst into tears. Now it was real. The likeness was unmistakable; same eyes, mouth and the distinctive oval shape of her face.

Grace Foster, age 51, living two towns away, listed as a postal worker. People living with or related to her were given as William J. Foster, aged 54, Laura Foster Kenner, age 24, and Kevin David Foster, aged 22.

Olympia started fanning through the directories and soon found her. The woman, with identical biographical information, had been a member of the church seven years ago, three years after D. E. Cameron was called to the church. Out of curiosity, she looked into the next two directories to see if she showed up there as well, but she did not. Come and gone without a trace—only she wasn't. She was living not a half hour from the church and almost an hour from where Olympia was sitting that very minute.

Olympia leaned forward on her elbows, cupped both hands over her mouth and stared at the unblinking screen in front of her. Now what?

She didn't know whether to be pleased or irritated when she heard the unmistakable *putter-rutter* sound of the canary yellow pickup coming into the yard. Either way, she knew damn well she wasn't going to get anything else done today. That was the irritation. Once she'd parked the research project in the to-do basket, she would be able to let it go until tomorrow. Now she could go and see what mischief Frederick had got himself up to.

"Cup of tea, my love?" The clipped English accent, the familiarity and comfort of an honorable man, the safety and security of the life she had chosen and was now living in the face of what she had just discovered momentarily overwhelmed her. She gulped.

"Oh, Frederick, I can't think of anything I would like more."

"Shall I bring it out there?"

"No, love. I need a break. Let's have it out in the conservatory, and you can tell me how your landscaping plans are developing. The sun's on the other side of the house now, so it won't be too hot to sit out there."

It was all so ordinary, so everyday plain and simple. Tea and biscuits on a summer afternoon. Two cats sleeping back to back in the sunshine.

BOING!!!! The clock on the mantle in the sitting room sounded a one-chime alarm, and there was a noisy, nosey house-ghost to complete the picture and make it all seem almost normal.

"Tea's up," called Frederick.

As she pushed back from her desk, Olympia felt a rush of gratitude for the simple gifts of home and hearth and man and cat and a concurrent wash of icy dread for the firestorm of fear and moral degradation which she was about to set into motion.

"Why me?"

Who else? The unspoken words hung in the silence.

FREDERICK, SENSING THE SOURCE OF HER DISTRESS, had added a few extra biscuits, which Olympia called cookies, to the assortment on the plate. Even though the day was warm, the hot milky tea worked its calming magic, and Olympia felt the tension in her neck and shoulders slipping away.

"The Englishman's cure for everything," he would repeat whenever he had the opportunity, "everything from hemorrhoids to a broken heart."

It never failed to make her smile.

"Let me guess, you've found one of the victims."

Olympia nodded. "No point going into the details. There's no doubt there will be more to come. I wonder how Jim's making out with the high tech police stuff. I got a match with Google Image Search. It took me less than a half hour. I've got a name, where she lives and where she works. You'd think I was a detective instead of a minister." She bit into her second cookie.

"If you ever retire, you could write mystery novels. Change the names, of course."

"Very funny." She reached for a third. "I suppose the next step is to go back and keep on searching. God knows how many more I'll find. After that I'm going to need some guidance as to how to approach these women."

"I'm sure Jim will have some ideas. With all that the Catholic Church has been through on the subject, and his police buddy's direct experience, there's probably a suggested protocol on how to approach a victim."

"A victim who's kept it secret all these years, a victim who doesn't know me from a hole in the ground, a woman I walk up to one day and offer to turn her life upside down free of charge. How the hell did I get so lucky?"

Frederick ignored the sad sarcasm and said simply, "We only get to choose some of our battles, my love. The others are thrust upon us out of nowhere, and we can choose to stand and fight or we can choose to stand aside and hope someone else will take up the flag and the sword. I know you too well, Olympia. You keep your flag and your sword ever to hand, and I love you all the more because of it."

"Why me?" she wailed for the second time that afternoon.

"Who else?" She'd heard that before, as well, and it called for a fourth cookie.

Jim didn't wait until after supper to call in. He'd found three matches, and Olympia had found a second living one and a third who'd died. One of his matches overlapped with one of hers, Grace Foster. Between them they had the names and faces of four damaged women.

"Do you think we have enough to get started?" she asked, not entirely hopefully.

"Probably, but I think we should go through the entire list before we do. If we learn as much as we can about the individual victims, we may be able to pick out a pattern here."

"Jim? This is starting to look and feel more like police work than ministry. Are we getting in over our heads? This man has committed multiple crimes. What did your policeman friend say about what we're doing?"

"He said we were building a case, and when we have as much evidence as we think we can gather, then we decide what to do with it. He's willing to see us ... on the QT, of course."

"But Jim, both us have a duty to warn. We are mandated to report abuse of any kind, even beyond the curtain of the confessional."

"I asked him that very thing. He told me these are past crimes. They are not happening now. If they were, our reporting them would or could put a stop to them or at the very least interrupt them. But once they are history, in this case years, it is up to the victims to open an inquiry or make an accusation or seek justice after the fact/ex post facto."

"And that almost never happens ..."

Jim finished the sentence for her, "without an ally or an advocate."

"Damnhellshitcrap." It was her new favorite four letter word.

"My sentiments exactly. The reality is that they may or may not want to speak up. And I warn you, Reverend Doctor Firebrand, if they don't want to, you/we have to leave them alone. We do not have the right to invade anyone's privacy."

"If that happens, then what?"

"Then we back off and draw up another battle plan, or we don't. In some cases victims don't open up at first, but given time to think about it, can sometimes change their minds and come back to the table."

"It's all so tenuous."

"It's people's lives, Olympia. Real people, next-door neighbors and their families, people who push shopping carts, not celebrities who have money and expensive lawyers. It's Joe and Josephine Ordinary who work in the bookshop down the street, or the local hospital or teach in the elementary school. It's their lives which will be savagely interrupted and tarnished when this comes out in the open. And it will be your little church's life and history and reputation blasted to kingdom come by the accursed newcomer. You are wading into very deep waters that won't like being stirred up, my friend, and there's no turning back now that you've started."

Olympia shivered at the enormity of what she'd set in motion when she started cleaning out the desk. What if she hadn't been the one who found the condoms and the pictures? There was no doubt that eventually someone would. Then what?

"I guess it's back to image search for the two of us. I'm really glad you showed me how to mask off and isolate the faces. I don't think I could stomach looking at the entirety over and over again."

"The thing is, Olympia, it's not about the sex, it's about power, one human having dominion over another and using that power first to coerce and then to control." Jim's voice broke. He cleared his voice and continued. "I never told you this, Olympia, but I was one of those altar boys you read about, one of the ones that got caught alone over and over again in the empty sacristy after the last mass."

"Oh God, Jim, I'm so sorry. Why didn't you tell me? I mean ..."

"Shame and rage, helplessness and rage, fear and rage, humiliation and lost innocence and shattered beliefs —and rage. If I had spoken up, no one would have believed me, and the only thing that would happen was that I'd get a vicious belt strapping for saying such a thing about The Father. You have no idea. We've got to help these women, Olympia. Nobody helped me and others like me. Everybody looked the other way and fiddled with their rosaries and left the lambs to the slaughter."

His voice was rising now, the long-buried fury coming to the surface in a white hot rush. "Maybe I want to help these women now because nobody helped me then. Maye it will help me deal more fully with my own past and exhume all the shame and the lies so that eventually they can have a proper burial."

Olympia had never heard Jim sound like this and wished she was present with him. "I'm so sorry," she whispered for a second time. It was all she could think of to say.

Before ending the call, Jim suggested she go back and see if she could find the obituary of the victim who had died and possibly learn anything about the cause of death.

"Tomorrow, Jim, I need a breather."

July 1867

I cannot explain the genesis of this evil tide of gossip, but earlier today, after the Sunday service, I heard the full and shameful extent of it from our Minister, Reverend Otis Meacham. He drew Susan and me into his office and told us of a growing suspicion on the part of some in town that we two have an unnatural friendship, and we are starting a school for girls because of that distasteful predilection. How utterly vile a thought. How cruel. I think now of my dear Richard (husband in name only,) and how he has suffered and must live in secret because of who he is. I continue to say our friendship is no one's concern but our own, but the gossip is shameful and most hurtful.

Reverend Meacham and I both agree it may be that behind the gossip is the shameful truth that some people in this town are displeased to see the growing number of negroes moving north after the end of the civil war. And more so is the idea of making such people equal to them through education is secretly unthinkable. But they dare not admit to that, so instead, they are attempting to stop me to prevent that from happening. What despicable hypocrisy they are spewing forth.

More anon, LFW

On Friday morning, with a cup of fresh coffee on the desk beside her, Olympia was back in her home office. The cats had been banished to the main part of the house because of their double propensity for taking inconvenient and determined naps on whatever was spread out in front of her.

She sighed and opened the membership directory to page one. Ella Adams. Now there's a fine old New England name, she thought. I will begin at the beginning and see what I can learn. But she was interrupted, this time by the sound of a multi-wheeled truck beeping and backing up the driveway and Frederick bursting into the office and apologizing because he'd forgotten to ask her to move her van, and could she possible do it now.

"What the hell is going on out there?"

"Oh, that. You mean the truck."

Olympia nodded. "Yes, husband, the black and

yellow dump truck. The one that is outside this very window."

"Well, you see, I ordered some rocks."

"Of course you did. Silly me not to have figured that out. Frederick, can you please tell me why we are having rocks, and by the look of them big rocks, delivered to the house."

"It's part of something I'm working on. I was hoping you'd be out when they were delivered."

"Well, obviously I'm not. Darling. Sweet lovely impetuous and mysterious Frederick, what the bloody hell are you up to?"

"Well it all started when I decided to build you a Koi pond in the back garden and surprise you, only the idea sort of expanded." He paused. "Uh, why don't I go move your van, and then after they dump the rocks, I'll tell you all about it."

I fear this is not going to end well, thought Olympia. Why does a back yard fish pond need boulders the size of a small car? Just what kind of fish is he thinking of getting? Whales? Swordfish? I won't ask you, my well-meaning love. Let me guess.

"Frederick, can we talk this over before they dump the rocks." It was not a question.

"But ..."

"They can't dump them until I move the car, and actually, I'm not going to move my car, I'm going to tell them there's been a planning board glitch, and we can't take delivery right now, but we will reschedule. By the way, did you ever call the planning board and get permission? You do need a permit, you know."

"Uh, I seem to have forgotten about that."

Couldn't be bothered, most likely.

Olympia did not storm out the back door. She shot out like a greased cannonball and screeched to a halt beside the truck. She took a deep and calming breath, then sweetly and in no uncertain terms explained the situation to the delivery men, thanked them for their service, saying that there had been a little mistake in communication, and firmly blessed them on their way.

When she came back into the house, Frederick was sputtering something about the planning board and where was it.

Olympia put her hands on her hips and squared her shoulders. "Frederick, when it comes to structural changes in the building or alterations of the immediate geography, I am the planning board ... or at the very least," she dropped her voice and softened her stance, "we both are, darling. We make major decisions together, remember?"

"But ..." Frederick, his color rising, was equidistant between frustrated and furious with the latter gaining speed. Frederick didn't get seriously angry very often, but he was fast approaching it.

"We'll talk about it later. I need some fresh air."

"I'm sorry," said Olympia. Her words hung in the empty air as Frederick reversed and pulled out of the drive.

She stayed, leaning on the counter in the kitchen, and considered the situation. She knew she'd not been sensitive and most certainly had overreacted. On the other hand, had she not intervened, they would have a load of boulders, all of them with an uncertain future, sitting in the back yard. She knew Frederick would come back in a couple of hours in a better frame of mind. She would repeat the apology and then, together, they would address the matter of the fish pond or Lake Erie or whatever the back yard was destined to morph into. As part of that conversation she would tell him that she was indeed surprised by his thoughtfulness, and might it be possible that together, they could even come up with something even more wonderful?

CHAPTER 23

"Davld Cameron up in 204 seems to be very agitated today. He keeps trying to tell me something, and poor man, he just can't get the words out."

Angela Hendryx, the CNA assigned to his unit, and Valerie Carosella the nurse manager, were having a quick cup of coffee before the residents would be collected and taken around to their morning activities.

"Did he eat his all breakfast?" asked Valerie

"If you mean did he eat what I spoon fed him, yes. He put away every bit. I have to say he's showing more interest in food than when he first came in." The soft Oklahoma accent rounded the edges of many of her words.

"That's not uncommon. None of them ever want to come here at first, and then something happens, and they settle in like they've been here since Adam was a pup.

Exactly when that happens is different for everyone, but for most of them, it eventually does. Then everyone feels better."

"I can tell you the PT is working pretty good. He's getting more mobility and control on his right side."

"How do you know?"

"I got a little too close to the hand that works, and the old buzzard tried to grab my butt." She grimaced. "I'm glad he's improving, but I totally hate it when they grab you—or worse."

"And him being a minister. You never know, do you? What did you do?"

"I told him in no uncertain terms to keep his dang hands offa me. Now I'm telling you." Angela's cheeks were getting red.

"You did the right thing. Put an instant stop to it. The guy's all there mentally, but physically he's basically gone."

"Not gone enough for me this morning," said Angela, "but he sure won't get a second chance."

"His family is coming in today for a consultation. Do you want me to say something to them?"

She thought for a minute and then shook her head. "I took care of it. It happens every so often. Some old guy thinks he still has a twinkle in his eye and decides to act on it. I took care of it. It isn't the first time, and it won't be the last."

"If you're sure …"

"I'm sure."

"Okay, then, but I will tell them about the agitation.

Maybe they can figure out what's going on. There might be something they know that we don't, some other ancillary problem."

"If you do find out, go ahead and fill me in, okay? I really do care about him, you know." She flashed a warm smile.

"You care about them all, Angela. I know that."

"I'll pray for him. It's not easy being here, especially when your mind is still pretty good and you bein' so physically helpless. He's a man of God, but he's still a man. Some men think they can do it right up until the end. We all know that."

The nurse manager nodded with a wry smile. "Or at least they keep trying."

"And being a good Christian woman, at least aiming to be, I'll always be compassionate and forgiving, but I'll also keep myself well out of arm's reach. Covering my, uh, bases, if you know what I mean."

"I do indeed," said Valerie, "That's why the residents love you so much. You have the perfect blend of dedication, deep personal faith and impish humor."

"Amen and thank you for the kind words." The kindly woman smiled, blushed, mock-saluted and left to go back to her unit.

———

THELMA AND SELMA WERE DOING WHAT THEY ENJOYED doing most: making plans. They were buttonholing volunteers and assigning them tasks and planning a vegetarian menu for Saturday. The sisters were in agreement about the new minister. So far, they liked her. Pastor Olympia could be just what their church needed. A breath of fresh air and a different energy, but not so much energy that she could upset the equilibrium built up over the years. True, no one could preach like Pastor Dave, he really had the gift, but over time the numbers continued to dwindle. Lots of people came through the doors, attracted at first by the power of the word, his word, but on more than one occasion, the person or the family just stopped coming. Never came back. Never a word of why. Nobody asked.

Curious, they told each other over their afternoon glasses of sherry. It really was a shame that churches didn't have exit interviews, the way businesses did. Before they retired both had worked in the corporate world, and they knew how business should be done. And really, wasn't a church just another kind of business?

An organization is an organization, and a marketing plan is a marketing plan. If any group, religious or secular, had a company policy, those explicit expectations of behavior and communication between labor and management could be found in a dusty handbook somewhere. Unopened.

Then there were the rules that everyone lived and worked by, those unstated expectations that a savvy newcomer could only learn if he or she watched, waited, didn't speak up too soon and asked the right people for advice.

Churches were much the same. Policies and changes to the by-laws were too often put in place after the crisis, more a theological BAND-AID or a palliative fix than prevention.

The sisters had, that very morning, over their morning oatmeal, discussed whether they might need to draft a dog or pet policy or at the very least a set of suggested guidelines for animals in the building. Not that they wanted a newcomer, any newcomer, more especially the most recent newcomer, to feel singled out or anything even remotely approaching it. No, this should be a general topic for future consideration and deliberation— in executive session, of course.

For over thirty years one or the other of them, and sometimes both at the same time, had been part of the congregational governance board of The South River Community Church. They'd never married, never had pets to dirty a house where even the plants knew their place and never dropped a petal or a leaf. In many ways the church was the child they never had. It was both family and social life for Thelma and Selma. It was years ago when they'd had taken it upon themselves to care for it and keep it safe, and a promise is a promise, come hell or high water. Ministers come and go. It's the church that stays.

Of course they'd heard the whispers and the mumblings about Pastor Dave and his after hour "counseling" sessions, but they steadfastly refused to give credence to single a word of it. As far as they were concerned, without proof it was all malicious lies and vicious, possibly even jealous, gossip, designed to bring down a man who was as handsome and charming and generous and caring as a pastor could be. It was true that his wife and children had left him shortly before he'd come to work at South River, but as far as they were concerned, that was her loss and their gain and nobody else's business. Any man, particularly a man of God, needs his privacy, and if this particular man of God had certain ... needs, these, too, should be private.

CHAPTER 24

On Friday morning after almost an hour of meaningless busywork, aka, procrastination, Olympia marched herself into her office and tapped Grace Foster's number into her cell phone. Her hand was shaking, and her heart was in overdrive.

"This is Grace."

Olympia did her best to make her voice sound bright and cheery. "Good morning, Grace. My name is Olympia Brown, Reverend Olympia Brown. I'm the new pastor at the South River Community ..."

"Sorry, Reverend, I don't mean to be rude, but I don't do church, which means there's no point carrying this conversation any further. It would be a waste of both our time. I'm sure you've got lots of call to make. So thank you, no thank you, I wish you a good day, and goodbye."

That's me told, thought Olympia, but she pressed on anyway.

"Please don't hang up. I'm the new minister at the South River Community Church. I'm trying to reach out to people whose faces I see in the directory but not in the pews. I wonder if …"

The line went dead, and the silence following the disconnect spoke volumes.

The next number she called, to a woman named Marigold Wilson, had been disconnected, no further information available. She had an address on that one. Maybe after what had just happened she would try writing a letter and use that as a way to start the conversation. "Dear Marigold, I found your name in an old directory, and I'm inviting you to come back and see us sometime."

She would, of course, keep copies of any written correspondence. She knew that a paper trail, hard copy or electronic, along with witnesses and corroborators was vital as credible evidence of suspected wrongdoing. What she lacked were victims. No, scratch that. She had victims. She needed victims who would talk to her. And then what? Call the next number on the list, Olympia.

The woman who answered yes, was Betty Almasi, and yes, she had been a member of South River for a couple of years, but that was ages ago. Quite frankly, that was then, and this was now and, long pause, she saw no reason to come back. When the woman didn't hang up, Olympia pressed on.

"As the new minister here, I'm trying to get a picture of the church as it was in comparison to what it is now. You do know that Pastor David Cameron is no longer here? He had a massive stroke, literally fell out of the pulpit and was carried out on a stretcher. I've just stepped in to try to hold things together." Olympia couldn't stop herself from thinking, *stepped in what?*

"I suppose I should say I'm sorry to hear that, but I'm not." A long pause. "Let's just say we didn't part under the best of terms, and I never went back. Good luck, Reverend, and even though I don't know you from Adam, I will tell you this: Be careful. That place is sick."

Bingo!

Olympia would not let herself become excited lest it become manifest in her voice. "Really. I would be very interested in hearing why you feel that way. I can assure you my absolute confidence if you care to elaborate on that. I'll be honest with you, I've heard some vague mutterings, but if I ask what happened, everyone goes silent."

"I've never told anyone what happened."

Olympia spoke softly and straight from the heart. "Would you like to tell me?"

An even longer pause. "Maybe."

Olympia was literally holding her breath.

"If the man is totally out of action, maybe I do. He can't hurt me now, or maybe I should say he can't hurt me anymore. Maybe it's because I don't know you, and sometimes it's easier to talk to a stranger than it is to someone you know. You know, like in bars or in airplanes, you pour your heart out to a stranger, knowing you never have to look at them again if you don't want to. So, yes, I think maybe I do want to talk about it."

Olympia quietly let out the breath she was holding onto for dear life.

"Do you think you might be willing to talk to me, Betty? At a coffee shop, maybe, someplace where you'd feel comfortable?"

Even though Olympia knew where the woman lived, she thought it best, at present, not to say so.

"I live in Middleborough. It's about an hour from the church. Where would you be coming from?"

"I live in Brookfields. There's a Panera off exit 7 in Plymouth that's just about halfway between us."

"Good old Panera, everybody's office away from home. I know it well. Give me a day and a time? I have a flexible work schedule."

"What do you do for work?"

"I'm a private nurse. I work under contract. Sometimes I'll take a case in a person's home, and sometimes I'll fill in at a local hospital for a couple of weeks. I still have teenagers at home, and I found that being unpredictable as to when and where I'll be at any given time does wonders in terms of keeping them in line. They just never know when Mommy is going to turn up, so they might as well behave."

Despite the gravity of the conversation, Olympia laughed out loud. "I sure wish I'd thought of that when I was bringing up my two sons. Still, we managed. They're out and on their own, and I survived. We all did. I'll tell you, though, they gave me a run for my money more than once. But we are getting off track, Betty. When is good for you? Mornings are best for me, just not Mondays. That's my day out of the office."

A pause. "Ah, yes, the office. The pastor's private study. Does it still lock from the inside?"

"Not any more, it doesn't. I think that after the next board meeting I'll have a better idea about what I'll be up against. However, that doesn't prevent us from sitting down together."

"I'm off Tuesday and Wednesday of next week."

"Let's say Wednesday at ten. Give me your cell phone number, and I'll give you mine in case something comes up."

"Pastor?"

"Yes, Betty?"

"I'm glad you called."

Olympia disconnected the call and leaned back in her office chair, thinking about the conversation and what that and the other conversations would unleash. I can only open the door, she thought. Each of them is free to enter in her own way—or not. There was no knowing.

She had experienced clergy abuse in her own life. Some years ago a predator pastor, an interfaith clergy colleague in a town where she was serving, had targeted her, but she'd managed to get away from him before it turned tragic. It left her badly shaken and the predator in jail. But that was the church across the street. This was her church, at least for the time being.

She'd never come into a church after a case of sexual misconduct before, and if she were to be honest with herself, she wasn't entirely sure she was qualified to step in. So-called "after pastors" were a breed unto themselves, clergymen and clergywomen specially trained to handle the institutional wreckage after such a situation. They knew how to address the broken trust, toxic shame and convoluted web of lies and dirty secrets following a pastor, most often a man, who uses his power and position to control and violate every aspect of the faith and trust placed in him. It was beyond despicable, and it was so goddamned common that clergy were now being trained to deal with it. What is it about churches? She'd asked this question many times, and no doubt would ask it again. All these years and still she didn't have a definitive answer. But this was what she had chosen to do with her life, and at this point the good still outweighed the bad. If the time ever came that it no longer did, then it would be time to walk away.

Pick your battles, Olympia. You are starting to make progress. Slow and steady, woman. Just keep going.

July 1867

Both the weather and my disposition are brighter today. Susan and I have met with Rev. Meacham, who is in full sympathy with my efforts, and it would appear that we may have the beginnings of a plan. He is a good man, and I am grateful for his support. And yet I must continue to ask myself, will the day ever come when a woman does NOT need the support of a man to realize her dream? Still, one does not look a gift horse in the mouth, does one? I will gather my hope where I find it.

More anon, LFW.

CHAPTER 25

Rayna Buxton came home from work early that afternoon. She was anxious to get back to her latest project. After going through the greeting ritual with her mother and the dog, she excused herself, saying she had a headache and needed to lie down for a while before starting supper.

"You work too hard, dear," said her mother.

"It's what keeps me going, Mum. If I never went out, nothing would ever get done now, would it?"

"But you don't really have to work. You could stay home with me and the dog. I'm getting better, you know. I could do some of the cooking. Why just today, I made my own lunch."

Rayna stopped halfway up the stairs. "You what?"

"I made my own lunch. I made a cheese omelet."

"You used the stove?"

"Rayna, I'm not a baby, even though you treat me like one sometimes. I was very careful, I used my rollator for balance and to carry things back to my chair, and I did just fine."

"Mother, I don't want you wandering around when I'm not here. You could fall. Then what would you do?"

"Silly girl. I'd push the red button on the medical alert bracelet you bought me for Christmas. Really dear, I'm not dead yet, but I'm beginning to feel that way."

"We'll talk about it later. I'm going to lie down for a little while. My back hurts."

"I thought you said you had a headache?"

"Same thing."

She left the door to her room open so she could hear if her mother needed anything and went straight to her desk. She was collecting information and material for her newest scrapbook project, Historic New England Churches. She'd always had an interest in local social and religious history, and she was a frequent and familiar visitor at local historical societies, records rooms at town halls and local libraries. Now that so much of what she needed for her research was on line, all she needed was a printer or a copy machine, a pair of scissors and a glue stick and she was good to go. The other details, the more complicated and time-sensitive stages of the project, would come later. Research first, carry-through later when the time was right.

One day all of this would be made available to the public and to other researchers and students of history and human behavior. Just not yet. She hadn't fully worked out the scope and the dimensions of the overall timeline. She did know that undertakings of this nature had a way of taking care of themselves and letting her know when they were complete. She'd researched three other local churches since she'd started doing this as a hobby; and meticulous as she was, she'd kept and filed every scrap of information, picture, copies of newspaper articles, even a selection of welcoming pamphlets from the churches themselves.

Rayna had a long-time interest in old churches. She loved the learning stories and history and the folk tales that were attached to them. She loved researching the stories behind the stories, because she'd learned long ago there were always stories behind the stories. Those were the ones she was really interested in.

Despite the fact that these projects of hers had begun to have a kind of sameness to them, Rayna continued to remain hopeful as she began each new one, hopeful that this would be the one that worked. Her mother used to say that crazy is doing the same thing over and over and expecting different results, but she wasn't crazy to keep on trying. She was being optimistic. She was creating a personal path to healing, and she'd keep at it until she got it right, and who in the world could argue with that?

Only she and her mother knew that she'd had several inpatient stays at a nearby mental health facility for anxiety and depression. That was history and not something she told strangers. Once they'd finally gotten her meds sorted out, she never went back.

CHAPTER 26

The welcome luncheon was scheduled for noon on Saturday. Now, getting ready and taking care to give herself plenty of time to be there well before noon, Olympia was considering the many layers of what she was heading into.

On the surface it was a straightforward meeting of the minds and a sharing of expectations. Under that heading she planned to ask the members what they had in mind for the next several months and what, if any, were the long-term goals or vision for the future. She would find a way to ask as much as she could about the previous ministry without sounding like she was prying. Standard questions, such as what worked over the years, and in particular in the last ministry, what they wanted to continue with, what needed work, and what might they want to change or add. Anyone starting a new job in a leadership position would and should ask these questions.

What she would be looking for would be the answers

underneath the answers, the silent language of sideways glances, evasions and telltale body language suggesting there was much that was not being said. Then what? She noticed she was asking this of herself a lot these days. That in itself spoke volumes. For one of the few times in her life, the way forward was not clear. She remembered having similar feelings all those years ago when Frederick kept pestering her to marry him. She was full of doubts but eventually decided to accept the challenge. And that worked out, didn't it?

South River was an entirely different kind of challenge, and Olympia was never one to be scared off by controversy or to be afraid to dive into troubled waters if the goal, after negotiating the rocks and the rapids, was worth it. Maybe she'd have that answer after her get-acquainted, goal-setting luncheon. It was time to get ready.

She chose a loose-fitting, off white linen tunic and pants outfit she'd scored at an end-of-season sale in one of the trendier shops on a visit to Martha's Vineyard. She liked wearing linen. It was supposed to look soft and sort of slept in. She added a flowery sash and a broad-brimmed sun hat, and she was the essence of casual chic and summer professional at the same time. She gave herself a thumbs up in the mirror and headed out the door.

Frederick blew her an air kiss as she went past. He had his own plans for the afternoon and was not at all unhappy that his lady wife would not be there to opine on how his liquid garden of Eden was about to unfold.

T HE ABSOLUTE LAST PERSON ON EARTH O LYMPIA
wanted to run into as she slid down out of her van was
Rayna Buxton, and yet there she was, Raggsy at her
heels, trotting toward the car carrying a large box.

"I called the church yesterday and learned there was
going to be a luncheon today, and the church would be
open. I decided to bring the cookies in early in case
something happened tomorrow and I couldn't get out."
She was beaming. "What's the luncheon for? Can
anybody come?"

Olympia started to reach down to pat Raggsy but
then pulled back, remembering Rayna's repeated
warnings.

"Oh, go on, he knows you now. It's okay. I only have
to tell him once. He's a dog, but he's got the memory of
an elephant. If you'll open the door for me, I'll bring
these cookies in and put them right into the fridge. I
already arranged them on plates. If you like I'll give you
the recipe. Even better, I'll make up some especially for
you."

Olympia smiled and swallowed a string of exception-
ally unclerical one-syllable words. "I'll get the door for
you, Rayna, and we can bring the cookies into the
kitchen. It's very kind of you. I'll make sure Thelma and
Selma know who brought them."

"I wrote my name on the box so they'll know who
made them."

Olympia thought she'd run out of four-letter words,
but as luck would have it, she hadn't. "As far as the lunch

goes, it's really a meeting of the governing board with food attached. All business, I'm afraid, and for just me and the board, but I will make sure you get a hand-written invitation to the next potluck supper. I understand these people are renowned for their potlucks."

Rayna didn't look convinced but put on her best brave-girl-who's-just-been- rejected smile and said, "Oh, all right. Will you really handwrite it?"

Olympia nodded and gently herded Rayna and the dog back out the door and into the sunshine. She did not ask how she got there, and she did not ask where she was going.

"See you tomorrow," Rayna chirped.

Not if I see you first! Olympia immediately chided herself for having such uncharitable thoughts and turned to go back into the church just as the twins in their shiny black Crown Victoria rolled into the parking lot.

Let battle commence, she thought, as she walked over to greet them and offer help carrying anything that might need it.

The rest of the members of the board arrived almost simultaneously, carrying baskets, bags and assorted covered platters. They were a merry bunch in the kitchen, chattering, unwrapping and arranging what looked to be a lovely and well-planned meal. Thelma and Selma directed operations, the flowers on their respective hats bobbing and keeping tempo along with their quick efficient footsteps.

Olympia, watching it all from the sidelines, was fighting the overwhelming urge to bolt, to run out to her car and simply send them an email of resignation when she got home. Of course she wouldn't, but when should she open such a difficult conversation? With the salad, after they'd fed her? Thank you for the lovely meal, and now I'm going to make you all want to throw it back up.

"My, my you're looking serious, Pastor. Got something on your mind?" Ted Jennings, the church treasurer interrupted her thoughts.

She brushed away his concern with a cheery smile. "One of those million-miles-away moments. I'm sorry."

"Hey, it happens. Come on, I think we are supposed to go in and sit down. Thelma and Selma have totally outdone themselves today. Will you look at all this?" He waved his arm in an expansive gesture indicting the carefully set table, the fresh flowers and the abundance of beautifully presented food upon it.

Olympia gulped and smiled. She felt like Benedict Arnold on steroids, the world's worst and most mean-spirited traitor. Only she wasn't. She would wait until after the meal and for the scheduled business part of the afternoon to speak her truth. After that, *quien sabe?* Meanwhile, she would not ruin the present, hers or theirs, with her troubled and troubling thoughts. They'd gone to so much work in her honor. She looked at the faces around her, saw their smiles, felt their hope and their generosity, and she gave thanks for the bounty and the goodness before them.

She would speak her truth, and she would do it thinking about the words of St Francis: She would seek to heal, not to hurt, to comfort where there was pain, and to bring light where there was darkness. God help me, and may God have mercy on my soul, she prayed silently.

Walking down the main street toward the part of town where she and her mother lived, Rayna was reviewing the events of the morning. Just as she was getting to know these people, all of a sudden she'd been turned away and rejected. It didn't matter what Pastor Olympia had said or how she'd explained about the business meeting thing. The bottom line was, they didn't want her. She was not invited to their special lunch. She was feeling hurt and confused, and when she felt hurt and confused she knew she was soon going to feel angry. It was a familiar pattern. Too Familiar. One that troubled her, because she knew where it would lead. Why was it always the same? Why did it always end up this way? Maybe her mother was right. Maybe she was crazy. She really had believed this time would be different. These people, especially the pastor, were all so nice. Well, the twins had a fit when Raggsy got water on the floor, but they got over it and even gave her some water. So maybe they were okay after all, just a too little protective of their shiny damn floor. Wasn't church about welcoming the stranger and comforting the afflicted? Besides, she'd only just started the scrapbook. She gave Raggsy's leash a companionable tug.

"Come on, dog. Let's see what tomorrow brings. I really shouldn't be so quick to judge, you know. It's a bad habit. Let's see what these people have to say for themselves after they try my cookies."

CHAPTER 27

At the end of the meal and before the meeting, everybody pitched in to help clear the table. Olympia insisted on being part of the operation right down to folding the tablecloth, brushing the leftover crumbs into her hand and tossing them in the trash. After a fifteen-minute freshen-up break, they reassembled around the table, this time with notebooks and writing materials. Present were the board president, Michael Nee; Selma, the moderator; and her twin sister Thelma, the scribe of the record and handwritten note taker; Laurel Ahearn, corresponding secretary and keeper of all things electronic; members at large, Ellen Brody and Jeanne Lane; Treasurer, Ted Jennings; Constance Mella and Olympia Brown. All traces of the festive luncheon had been removed, and now the table held bottles of water, writing materials, and their collective hopes and aspirations of securing a new minister. The countdown had begun.

Michael Nee, the president of the board, called for attention and then smiled in her direction. "Pastor Olympia, I'm sure it will come as no surprise to hear that we'd all like you to come and serve this congregation, and I believe you wouldn't be here if you weren't willing to come, so the only things that remain are the details." Another even broader smile. "And I'm sure those can be worked out in short order." Olympia cleared her throat. "If you don't mind, and before this can go any further, I'd like to take a few minutes to talk about something I found last Monday while I was working in the pastor's study."

The room fell dead silent, and every eye and ear was fixed on her. From the low, steady tone of her voice, they clearly knew whatever was coming was serious.

"What did you find, Pastor?"

She took a deep breath. "This is not going to be easy for any of us. Last Monday I came in to kind of clean up and sort out the office—you know, make some space for my own things, settle in a little bit. When I lifted an organizer in the top drawer, I found an empty condom wrapper and two unused ones." She held up a warning hand over the mounting outcry. "Wait, please. Unfortunately for all of us, there's more. In the bottom left hand drawer I found an envelope containing a number of sexually explicit photographs showing David Cameron with a variety of female partners."

Over the gasps and cries of shock and outrage, came Michael Nee's voice. "Go and get them, please."

"I don't have them with me."

"We need to have them. They belong to us." Nee held out his hand.

Olympia stood her ground. "They are safe where they are, and technically they probably belong to David Cameron. Do you really want to claim them as church property? What matters now is not who they belong to or who has the rights to them, but the fact that they exist at all. What I have is visual evidence of repeated acts of sexual congress, very likely abusive, committed by your previous minister."

She paused for a quick breath in the stunned silence that fell over the room. "Until we address this awful reality, there can be no going forward for any of us—not you as a church, and not me as a minister to this church."

"But ..."

"Oh no."

"I can't believe ..."

"You have to hand them over." Nee's voice was rising.

Olympia stood her ground. "I repeat, I don't have them with me, and like it or not, we need to address this right here and right now. It's likely there are some of you in this church who had no idea of what has happened. I am also quite certain there are people who strongly suspected it and for any number of reasons, fear of public shame being the most prevalent, have denied it and have remained silent. As hard as this is to say, and it is not a direct accusation of anyone here in this room, but historically in these situations, there are people who knew exactly what was going on and purposely said nothing."

She paused for another breath and the courage to

continue. "Now I am going to beg you, please do not shoot the messenger. Trust me, I am not happy about finding these items. What I am asking you is that you speak the truth about what you know and when you first knew it, here and now or later, privately with me in the study. Curiously, it may be better that I'm not well known to you. I've only been here for a little over a week, and I don't have a history with you. In some ways that alone might make this a little easier for us all. Furthermore, I give you my solemn word that I will say nothing of this outside these walls."

"We still need to have those pictures."

Olympia held up her hands and carefully did not raise her voice. "This is not about the pictures. It's about what they represent. It's about what happened here and continued to happen over a period of years and about why no one spoke up. The Roman Catholics are struggling with the very same thing."

"We're not Catholic. We're not like them. This wasn't little kids … was it?"

"Oh my God," wailed Jeanne Lane.

"We can't let this get out, it will destroy the church."

As the defensive and accusatory din rose up around her, Olympia was taking careful notes, watching and listening to who was speaking up, who was crying out in anguish—and who was remaining silent.

Olympia let the outrage cry itself out. She waited until there began to be spaces in the conversation, and the men and women around the table began to look in her direction. Finally a voice rose above the others. It was

Constance Mella, the keeper and custodian of the building and its local history.

"Look here, everybody. The way forward is clear. The man is gone, whatever happened is history, and please note that I haven't seen the so-called evidence myself." She stopped and glared at Olympia, "And until we do, we have to take your word for it, and who the hell knows what axe you have to grind? I move that we rescind any offer we might have made to this woman here and ask her to leave the premises immediately. If she does say anything, it's her word against ours. People can do anything with computers these days. I say the so-called evidence is fake, and so is Olympia Brown. Spawn of the devil, she is." She was getting louder and redder. "Thou shalt not bear false witness against thy neighbor. What kind of a Christian are you?"

One of the elected members-at-large, Ellen Brody, stood up. She was white faced and gripping the chair in front of her for both physical and moral support. Olympia knew her face and her first name, but not much more. She was not one of the coffee ladies. The woman let go of the chair and held up her hand for silence.

"Hold it, all of you. I can tell you for a fact that Pastor Olympia is not lying. It's true. It did happen. I know one of the women he abused, and she is terrified of ever being found out. I will never reveal her name. After Cameron had the stroke and was gone, she called me and told me what happened, and she told me about a picture he took of her. He told her that if she ever uttered a single word about what happened, he would say she was the one who came on to him, and she sent the picture to him as an invitation."

She stopped for a moment to collect herself and then continued. "I always wondered why she stopped coming with never a word about why, but when I asked, she said it was because she never felt as though she fit in. And I have to ask the question. Why did she feel she didn't fit in, because there was not one person in this whole congregation she could trust enough to say what happened to her? And if that is the case, what in God's name are we, because we're damn sure not a church?" Ellen shouted her final words, then, covering her face with her hands, she and fell back into her seat, her whole body shaking.

Olympia listened intently and remained silent.

After a long and painful silence, Constance stood and clasped her hands together in a gesture of humility. "I need to apologize to you for my harsh words, Pastor. I did try and shoot the messenger, and I am deeply sorry for it."

All eyes were on her, waiting. She collected her thoughts and chose her words. "Your feelings are completely understandable. There is nothing worse for any church congregation than what you have all collectively experienced, both now and in the years leading up to this moment. You are shattered, one and all, for your own reasons, and I won't ask what they are right now. I will say to you that one day you will need to address this amongst yourselves. Clergy sex abuse, despicable as it is, is far more common than any of us would like to think, and when we do think or speak of it, it's to point a finger at the church over there and not at ourselves."

More people were crying now. Some were holding hands. Others were sitting in a stunned, wide-eyed silence as Olympia continued speaking. "Sad as it is to say, this despicable behavior is common enough that professional church leadership institutes have created special training programs for clergy and counselors who feel called to this unique and challenging ministry. Men and women who come in after an abusive situation and guide a congregation through the healing process. When you feel ready, I will put you in contact with these wonderful people.

"Churches can and do survive this, but I have to warn you, the cure is every bit as excruciating as the disease, and it takes real courage and commitment as a whole congregation go through it and come out the other side."

"What about tomorrow," wailed Selma? "It's Sunday. What are we going to do?"

Once again, all eyes turned to Pastor Olympia. She spoke more gently now. "While I am no advocate of toxic secrecy and silence, neither am I an advocate of starting a fire to clean out the underbrush until everybody agrees on where to start it and how to manage it once it is started. What I suggest is that you hold this in your shared confidence for now and then schedule another meeting as soon as you can with a trained facilitator to start the process of clearing and healing."

They were still looking at her, waiting. "If you want me to, I will be back in the pulpit tomorrow, and I will plan to stay on and help until such time as we find the right facilitator for your own recovery. Meanwhile, I cannot stress the importance of keeping this confidential for now with the solemn promise of full disclosure in the future. We need to be done with the covering up."

"Can't we just keep you?"

"One challenge, one truth, one day at a time. Let's get through tomorrow first and let me look into my resources for an After Pastor for you."

"But what if we want you. What if we all agree and vote on it?"

"I won't say yes, but I won't say no. I repeat, let's all just get through tomorrow. Meanwhile, would you please join me in prayer?"

CHAPTER 28

When Olympia got home she dragged herself though the door and walked, zombie-like, into the sitting room and melted into her chair. Her exhaustion was so viscerally evident that even the cats kept their distance. Frederick, who was working in the garden when she arrived, came into the house to see how it went. One look at her sprawled form said it all.

"That bad?"

"Beyond bad. When I first told them what I'd found I thought they'd have a collective heart attack. Shock, rage, denial, accusation, guilty looks, the whole works. But in the end they did not burn me at the stake or ride me out on a rail. They started to listen."

"What turned the tide?"

"The credible words of another victim—anonymous, of course, but told to a trusted friend and, as it turns out, a woman who happens to be a member of the board."

"Crikey."

"In a word. After that it was total and complete chaos while they tried to take in what they were hearing. It took some time, but eventually they calmed down enough and were able to hear me and listen to each other."

"And now what?"

"Predictably, they wanted a quick fix … have me stay on, never mention it again and make it all go away. I said I would come back tomorrow, but they needed more help with healing than I could provide on a long term basis. I think they heard the words 'come back tomorrow' and understood them to mean I would stay on. But they've had enough reality for one day. The last thing they need to feel is totally abandoned and cast adrift. I'm in for the short-haul, and I'll stay there until we find the right fit for the long one."

"Crikey."

"You are starting to repeat yourself."

"Ahhh, I think I detect improvement. Say, why don't I make supper tonight?"

Uh oh. "Um, well now, what were you thinking of making?"

"Reservations, my love. You need a night off."

"I still have to write a sermon."

"Okay then. Plan A is we go out now, have an early dinner, you don't have any wine, and we get you back in time to write your sermon."

"What's Plan B?"

"You get started right this minute, and I'll come get you in three hours, and you can have wine with the meal."

"Plan B."

Olympia took herself off to her office. She was running on empty and struggling to write a sermon that encouraged, but did not inflame, that spoke the truth but not too much of it and that suggested that "the times they are a-changin'" big time. They needed to keep the faith and remember that "in God we trust." She had her work cut out for her, but the promise of a good meal with a man she loved, and a glass or two of really nice wine, spurred her on.

AT THE VERY SAME TIME THAT OLYMPIA WAS TRYING TO construct her sermon, the powerful and self-appointed inner circle of the South River governing board was having an emergency private meeting. They were gathered in the very room where they'd recently had the welcoming luncheon for Pastor Olympia Brown. The atmosphere was tense, the mood was grim, and the power brokers were all determined that the disturbing and inflammatory information which had just been released to them would never see the light of day.

Thelma and Selma, moderator and scribe respectively, President Michael Nee and Ted Jennings, the treasurer, knew they had everything to lose and nothing to gain if this got out. This church represented everything their families had worked for and accomplished over the generations, and now, a dirty, embarrassing scandal could be the end of them.

By now they were all in agreement that Pastor Olympia was not to blame. She had done what any man or woman in her position would be expected to do; she brought it to the attention of the board. They only wished she had come to them first. Things could have gone differently. But as it was now, with the whole board aware of what had happened, it was up to them to steer the ship back into port with as few ripples as possible.

Theirs was a historic church. It mirrored the town's history back to the Civil War. Church and town had grown and prospered with the development of its industrial and manufacturing community. The people who had been instrumental in its mission and development were the leading families in the town. Over the generations these people had served the town in one capacity or another since it was incorporated, and while their words and opinions were not law, they came pretty damn close. Now the church that had been the social and moral compass in the town of South River was threatened with the very worst kind of scandal. They would deal with this. These people knew how to get things done.

Step one was to get control of the board. Step two was to make a call on Ellen Brody and convince her of the wisdom of letting sleeping dogs lie. Step three was to keep Pastor Olympia right where she was and convince her they were doing everything possible to make things right. And no way in hell were they going to bring in some goddamned expert who was going to tell them what to do. They knew how to keep things quiet, didn't they?

God knows they'd had plenty of practice.

CHAPTER 29

W hen Olympia and Frederick came back from the restaurant, the message light on the house phone was blinking. Olympia hit the play button while Frederick set out supper for the cats.

"Pastor Olympia, this is Ellen Brody. I'm the woman who spoke up at the meeting today. Could you please give me a call back? I'll be up at least until ten, tonight, and if you're not back by then, perhaps tomorrow morning before you leave for church. My cell phone number is …"

Olympia was grateful she'd had only one glass of wine with dinner, and that was two hours and a big meal ago. "It's the woman who came forward in the meeting. I'll make the call in my office."

"This seems to be the gift that keeps on giving," quipped Frederick. "Do you want a cup of tea? Herbal?"

"No, thanks, sweetheart. Any more liquid tonight,

and I'll be wearing out the rug between the bed and the bathroom."

Seated at her desk so she could take notes more easily, Olympia listened to the message again and hit redial.

"Ellen, this is Pastor Olympia calling." Olympia wondered whether she'd ever get used to that title. Did she want to? South River was the first and only church she'd ever served that called her "pastor."

"Thank you so much for calling me back."

"Thank you for speaking up today. It could not have been easy."

"That's an understatement, but when I saw what was happening in there, they were attacking you, and I knew you weren't lying. I'll tell you something else, after you said what you did, told us what you found, I think there might be another one."

"I'm not surprised. Do you think she might come forward?"

"She took her own life a couple of years ago. I never could understand why. Now maybe I do."

Olympia felt as though she'd been punched. "This is even worse than I thought." She paused. "Look, do you think the woman you mentioned might talk to me if she's guaranteed anonymity?"

"I can only ask."

"I hope she can, but either way, can you and I meet somewhere and talk early next week? I have no idea how this is going to play out. Only the victims can press charges, and I agreed to hold my peace until the church decides how they want to move forward."

"Don't hold your breath on that one, Pastor."

"What do you mean?"

"Let's just say that in all the years I've been a member, change, if it happens at all, is glacial in speed."

"Do you mind if I ask why you kept attending, even went on the board?"

"It's where I grew up. It's the only show in town for me, and I guess I believe in the bigger message and not the person delivering it. Maybe I thought I could make a difference. I never did like Pastor Dave. He was a flirt and a showman, but the old ladies lapped it up."

"We need to talk in person, Ellen, but I need to get Sunday out of the way and see which way the board is heading. Let's talk again early next week."

"Works for me."

"You may not believe me when I say this, but we are doing holy work. I just wish it were easier, but it rarely is."

"Thank you, Pastor. I'll be really interested in hearing what you have to say in your sermon tomorrow."

Olympia chuckled softly. "I'm not joking when I say that sometimes a sermon can be a moving target. You might think you have it nailed down and then everything shifts. You can tell me after the service whether or not I hit it."

As she came out of the office and back into the main house, she could hear the clock clanging and boinging in the empty sitting room. This was not a social call. Miss Winslow wasn't kidding.

"Warning noted, I'll be careful," she called out as she passed by the open door.

"Boing."

"All right, already, I heard you! I know I'm in over my head, but I do know how to swim. Remember?"

ON THE OUTSKIRTS OF SOUTH RIVER, RAYNA WAS having a difficult night. Her mind was full of questions and effectively pushing the possibility of sleep completely beyond reach. Part of her wanted to stop right there, abandon the new project, burn the scrapbook and look for a new one. Part of her wanted to strike out and make those South River people sorry for not welcoming her and her good intentions the way she wished they had. And still another part of her struggled against the first two, and this was a first. She felt she might actually have formed some kind of a bond with Pastor Olympia. The woman was kind, and she listened, and she loved animals. It was clear that Raggsy liked her, and he was unerring in his judgment of character.

At three in the morning and again at four-thirty, as the sky began to grow light outside her window, she still didn't know if she and Raggsy would go to church that morning.

At six, when the sun was fully up, Rayna pulled herself out of bed and went over to her desk.

CHAPTER 30

July 1867

The sky overhead is dark and threatening rain. This, along with winds that could easily lift the hat from my head, suggest there is a mighty storm brewing off to the west. Little Sammy, the cat, is restless as well. I am convinced animals know many things that we do not. Nonetheless, impending storm or not, we have good works to accomplish.

Pursuant to our efforts to educate women, Reverend Meacham has invited The Reverend Olympia Brown to make her way here from her church in Weymouth Landing, and preach in our very own pulpit in Brookfields this coming Sunday. It has been quietly agreed upon amongst us that she will address the divine mission in working for equality in education and suffrage for all. Following that, we will host a most generous collation in her honor. And then, when all present are full and well disposed, we will announce our intention for establishing The Brookfields Parish Day School for girls and young women.

Meanwhile, the wind is rising, and the sky has taken on a positively greenish hue. I must collect Sammy and the children.

More anon, LFW

OLYMPIA SIGHED, REPLACED THE SHREDDED RIBBON that served as a book mark and closed the diary. She'd been up since five and thought that reading a few pages of Leanna Faith Winslow's diary would be relaxing, and she might even doze off in her chair. Didn't happen. She could hear Frederick making getting up noises and decided this was as good a time as any to get the teakettle boiling and fire up the coffee pot. The cats, sensing purposeful movement on the part of their humans, appeared as if by magic in front of the cupboard where she kept the treats.

"You two are not as dumb as thinkle peep." It was a kind of spoonerism compliment she was fond of inventing. She dropped a few treats at the feet of each feline. "First things first."

Considering how little sleep she'd had, she told Frederick when he asked that she felt "not as bad as all that and better than expected."

"Whatever that means," said her husband, giving her bottom a friendly squeeze. "Did you finish your sermon?"

"With minutes and ellipses to spare. Should be interesting."

"What's the title?"

The scent of fresh coffee permeating the air around them was beginning to lift her spirits. "Well, I thought about, 'The Poisoned Well,' and then I thought, 'May-day-Mayday,' and then I thought about 'Chicken Little meets Humpty Dumpty.'"

"And?"

"I fell back on the familiar, 'Sex, Lies and Rock and Roll.'"

"Reverend!" He clapped his hand over his mouth.

"Okay." She held up her right hand in the Boy Scout salute. "I am speaking on 'Beloved Community.' Words used by MLK. It's broad enough that I can take it anywhere, but the real message will be that Beloved Community is a journey, not a destination. It is a moving, living thing that ebbs and flows with the times and the people. I will make no direct reference to the previous pastor's indiscretions, but I will end with asking people to think about where they are in the journey and remind them that transitions, difficult as they sometimes can be, offer all of us a chance to regroup and refocus."

"Not bad for a woman."

Olympia fired a wet dishcloth at him and scored a direct hit. "That's why I get the big bucks, boyo, and don't you forget it."

WHEN SHE ARRIVED AT THE CHURCH LATER THAT morning, a full hour before the scheduled start of the service, the place was already filling, and you could slice the tension in the air with a bread knife. She could only hope and pray that the board members had kept silent. If they had broken their word, she would pack up and leave that afternoon.

She headed toward the pastor's study, not at all sure she even wanted to step over the threshold, but step over it she did and stood rooted to the spot. The room had been stripped of everything but the desk and the chairs. The bookcase was bare as a bone. Even the rug, the curtains and the dust had been removed.

"Like it?"

She turned to see Thelma and Selma standing arm in arm behind her, smiling broadly.

"After what you told us yesterday, about what you found...and after all that, saying you would actually stay on, we thought it was the least we could do for you. We got a crew, and we came in last night and cleaned the place out like a dish, scraped it clean. You deserve a place of your own. Now you can do it up any way you want."

Olympia saw through this as quickly as you could say "plate glass window." They had really been looking for further evidence, and if they'd found it, she would be the last person to know.

"Why, I'm speechless." She really was.

"It didn't take as long as we thought. We even went out for Thai food afterward to reward ourselves."

"Where is everything that you emptied out? Some of it was church history and parish records. You don't want to get rid of that."

"It's safe. We took anything that looked important home with us," said Selma. "We'll go through it when things settle down. We'll take good care of it, don't you worry. Now the place is all yours. We should have done this for you before you got here, but things happened so fast."

Olympia held up her hand. "It was never a problem, just a bit dusty, that's all. Anyway, thank you so much, and if you'll please excuse me, I need to prepare for this morning's service. Could one of you open the windows and get the fans going in the sanctuary? Oh, and will you get one of the men to come and take these two, as well? It's probably like an oven in there already." She pointed to the two fans that had survived the office purge.

"Sure thing, Pastor. Can't have that, now can we?"

Olympia hung onto her smile until the door was fully shut behind them and gave silent thanks for the sixth commandment, "Thou shalt not kill," well, murder, actually, because otherwise in that explosive moment, she might have easily done something ugly. It was going to take every bit of her ministerial strength and fortitude to get through the next three hours, but come hell or high water, come a woman with cookies pulling a dog, come marching twins with matching hats, or even JC himself, she would do it. Maybe, when she was able to see the other side of all this, she would write that book, but who would believe it? She already had the title: Parish Ministry—Stranger than Fiction.

FORTY-FIVE MINUTES LATER, WEARING HER SUMMER clerical robe, she thanked the Ahearn family, Laurel and Josh, who would serve as ushers and take up the collection, and their children, Daelan and Payson, who would light the candles at the beginning of the service and extinguish them after the benediction.

Then humming "Onward Christian soldiers

marching as to war," under her breath, Olympia walked with a strong and purposeful step down the center aisle and ascended into the octagonal mahogany pulpit.

Minutes later, during the opening prayer, everyone present heard a loud pop, followed soon thereafter by a strong smell of smoke and the insistent shriek of the smoke detectors, followed by the voice of Olympia Brown, speaking clearly into the microphone, commanding that someone call 911 and adding they all needed to vacate the building immediately. "Go quickly to the exit nearest you. Please, those of you who are more able bodied, help those who are less so. Please go to the back of the parking lot and gather together under the shade tree."

CHAPTER 31

Thelma and Selma were already heading for the door and wailing. Ellen Brody took competent charge of the exodus, calming and herding the frightened congregants ahead of her like a well-driven snow plow. The smoke was getting thicker now, and Olympia headed for the door. She was the last out and the last to join the others under the tree as the first red truck came howling around the corner. She was counting heads and got to thirty-two when she realized that Rayna and Raggsy were not among them. Then she remembered not seeing them at the start of the service.

When the building was fully vacated, Ellen came over and stood beside Olympia. "I think we're all present and accounted for. I ran back in and did one last sweep. We're good."

Olympia thanked her and then bellowed above the din, "We need to stay back and keep out of the way. You all need to go home. There's nothing we can do right now."

Many were openly crying and holding onto one another. One or two were taking cell phone photos and videos when the flames shot through the roof, but not a person there made a move to leave.

Olympia was not keeping track of time. In essence, time had stopped for all of them, and thus she was surprised and profoundly grateful see Frederick running toward her.

"I heard it on the radio." He moved in close and put a protective arm around her shoulders. By now, she and the board members were clustered together well back and out of the way, watching as the firefighters slowly gained control of the conflagration.

And then, who knew exactly when, it was over and the Fire Chief, David Taylor was walking toward Olympia and the members of board.

"I'm inclined to think it was probably started by an electrical overload." He pointed back towards the still smoldering building. "Happens in hot weather like this with the AC and the fans all going at once. Everything's fine until somebody turns on the microwave and the coffee maker at the same time and boom, she's off and running. Old wiring, dried out building. It's a miracle we were able to knock it down. There's damage along the wall where it started and the roof above it, but I think you might be able to save a good part of it. Miracle really." He shrugged. "Maybe it isn't." He pointed toward the sky. "Maybe somebody was looking out for you.

Shame to lose all that history. I was married in this church."

By the time Frederick kissed his wife goodbye and left for home, the insurance adjusters were already circling around the shaken congregation like vultures salivating over a new kill. Ted Jennings took command of that situation, and in no uncertain terms, he advanced upon them and warned them off.

"Gentlemen and ladies, I do thank you for your evident concern, but we are fully insured, and we have our own people to handle this. We don't need you now, nor will we in the future, and if there is any mistaking my message, let me put it another way." He pointed toward the street, "Leave now!"

Michael Nee called the people that were still standing there, many in shock, closer to him and announced they would be holding an emergency meeting that afternoon at The Fosselbergs' home, and he would be in touch with them all as soon as they had worked out a plan. He was about to turn away when Rabbi Silverman from Congregation Beit Yaakov stepped forward, stood beside him and raised his hands in welcome and in blessing.

"Brothers and sisters, we worship on Friday night and Saturday. On Sunday our building is yours, if you want it. *Mi casa, su casa.*" He chuckled. It's an old Jewish saying. Just say yes, and we can work out the details later. We're landsmen, remember. Countrymen. We're all countrymen and women. This is our land."

And that's when Olympia burst into tears. This was her sermon for today, "Beloved community."

"Thank you, Rabbi," said Lesley Ruth. "I … I don't

know what to say."

The rabbi shrugged. "Say nothing. Look up the word *mitzvah*. It's a good deed, an act of kindness done quietly and without fanfare. It's what we do."

Olympia wiped her eyes, thanked the rabbi and turned to Thelma and Selma. 'I don't know how to get to your house. I'll need directions."

Thelma floundered but only for a moment. "Here, I'll write down the address. I'm assuming you have a GPS on your phone." She fumbled for a pen. "Of course, you do understand it will be mostly business, insurance, securing the building. We're still in shock. You might want to wait."

Olympia shook her head. "No. If I'm going to be with you for the foreseeable future, then I need to be with you today. What time?"

There was no mistaking the line she'd drawn in the sand, and if Thelma was less than pleased, she never missed a beat. "That's very kind of you, Pastor."

"I second the motion." Olympia turned to see Ellen standing beside her, giving her and the board a thumbs up.

"We might need to postpone our other conversation," whispered Olympia.

Ellen responded in an equally *sotto voce*. "I'll call you tomorrow or Tuesday. I do believe we're going to be in for one hell of a ride over the next few days."

"I'm in for the long haul. I've got my big girl spurs on."

"Good thing," said Ellen. "I think you're gonna need 'em.",

CHAPTER 32

Rayna Buxton almost choked on her second cup of coffee when she heard the breaking news about the fire at the South River Church coming over the TV. Earlier that day, even though she'd already left off the cookies, she made a last minute decision to forego church today and go walking off on her own for a couple of hours. Later in the week she'd ask to visit with Pastor Olympia privately and try and sort out her thoughts about church in general and her feelings about South River in particular.

When she returned she heard the news of the fire on the mid-day news. Her first thought was to hope and pray that no one was hurt, especially Pastor Olympia. She was different from the others. Her second thought was to go and see it for herself.

"I have to go out, Mum."

"But you just got back."

"I know, I forgot something at the store. I won't be long."

"That's all right, dear. I feel a nap coming on. Are we still playing Scrabble when you get back?"

"It's Sunday, Mother, Scrabble Sunday. Of course we will. Now you rest up so you'll be ready for me. Raggsy, you stay here take care of Mama, okay?"

She was already tapping open the Uber app as she ran out of the front door. Ordinarily, she'd walk. It was good for her. It helped her clear her head when her troubling thoughts threatened to get out of control, but today time was of the essence.

When she arrived at the church, only one fire truck remained, and Olympia and the last of the board members were getting ready to move on.

"Pastor. Oh, thank God you're all right."

"No one was hurt, Rayna, and we still don't know the extent of the damage to the church, but … Rayna, you've got hair. It grew back. When did that happen?"

Rayna clapped her hand to her head. She was not wearing her hat.

The woman never missed a beat. "Oh, that. I've had hair for a while now. I think I just got used to wearing the hat. You know, old habits. Still haven't found a hair style I like. It's still one day at a time with this cancer thing."

"Well, I think it looks nice, and much as I'd like to, I can't stay and talk just now. We've got to go deal with the insurance and the disaster restoration people. As soon as I know where, or even if, I can set up shop and get back to the pastoring business, I'll call you next week, and we can make a time to get together."

"You'd call me?" She looked completely dumbfounded.

"Well, of course I would. Why wouldn't I? Whether you were here or not when the fire broke out, you are here now, and you probably want to talk about it. I know you are on the mailing list, so I have your number. But I'll be wanting to meet with you and every single member and friend of the congregation. We need to hold on to each other right now, maybe more than ever before."

"Wow." Rayna Buxton was unconsciously running her fingers through her not-very-short brown hair. "Thank you, Pastor. I never thought of it that way before."

CHAPTER 33

Before leaving for the meeting, Olympia had had a final word with the head of the disaster clean-up team and also with Constance Mella, and Ted Jennings, representing the board of directors. Shaken as they were, they still had their heads about them and were asking precise questions, taking copious notes and snapping endless pictures of the sodden mess as they picked their way over, through and around it.

It was soon apparent that there was more structural damage than originally thought. The fire had spread through the electrical lines along the far outside wall all the way to the kitchen, but it stopped short of the offices and the church parlor.

"It's a damn good thing we upped the insurance when we did," said Ted. "I'm looking at all of this and listening to what the experts here have to say, and I'm already thinking there might be a way to declare it a total loss and then decide how we want to rebuild. I'm thinking it might be cheaper in the long run."

Constance put up a palm-out stop sign. "Hang on, Ted, we're talking history here. This place goes back to the time of the civil war. I think we should preserve everything we possibly can. Don't forget, if the insurance doesn't cover it completely, we can always use or borrow against the endowment. What is it up to now? Must be over a million, maybe even two. You must know, you're the treasurer."

"Well, uh, I don't keep a ledger in my head, but I can certainly look it up. Either way, the whole board has to approve, then the congregation has to vote. We may not even live that long. Think of the meetings." He clapped a hand to his forehead.

"Look, Ted, I don't think this is funny, not a bit of it. Can you save your humor for later? We're going to need it. Just not now, okay? To quote my salty grandfather, 'I'm feeling like something that's been shot and missed and shit at and hit.'"

"Now who's joking?"

"Okay, one for one. Let's get back to business. They are going to want a preliminary report."

"Not to mention the newspapers. One of the local reporters asked me if I thought this might be related to those other church fires."

"What other church fires?" Ted looked perplexed.

"According to the reporter there have been three other fires in nearby churches which have some disturbing similarities. All started on a Sunday. All looked accidental until they started investigating further and found evidence of possible arson."

"Really." Ted was repeatedly wiping his face and neck with a crumpled handkerchief. He was sweating profusely now, no doubt from the exertion of climbing over the rubble and his mounting awareness of the extent of the damage.

"Right now, this sure looks like an accident. It doesn't take an electrical engineer to figure out that we must have overloaded the circuits with all those fans and stuff. Who'd a thought? I damn sure didn't. We've used multiple fans before, never had a problem."

"We know the wiring is old, probably very dried out, and more than likely pretty mouse chewed. I'm not going to say I told you so, but the building and grounds committee has been trying to get money for new wiring for years, but no one wanted to touch the endowment. I say, let's get the final report from the disaster people and take it to the board. If they say we need to hit the endowment, we hit the endowment. What the hell else is it there for?"

"It's a hedge against the future. That's why we don't touch it."

Constance was losing patience. "Hold on now. Just where do you think you are going with this? Without a church to go to on Sunday, we have no future. We might as well set up in an empty store in a strip mall. At least there'd be plenty of parking and probably a doughnut shop next door."

"I think we need to talk to restoration people, the insurance people and maybe even the fire chief before we get back to the board. No sense getting worked up over something we don't know yet."

She nodded. "Amen to that. Sorry about the flash. I'm feeling pretty emotional right now."

Ted waved it away. "We all are, my friend. We all are."

THE EMERGENCY MEETING AT THE FOSSELBERGS' house, minus the members still at the site, was already in progress when Olympia arrived at the door. Selma thanked her for coming and ushered her into a living room that looked like it could have been taken straight from a setting of *Victoriana Magazine*. Massive shiny mahogany furniture, flowered drapes, an oriental rug, and a multitude of old family pictures arranged on the shawl-draped piano. There was a cut glass brandy service on a side table against the wall with a pair of silver candelabra standing guard on either side. If there was any dust in the place, it was lost in the carved roses on the furniture. The only decorative anachronism was a massive oscillating floor fan doing its measured best to move stale air over and around the assembled mourners. Because that's what they were, mourners, recently bereft of something that felt like family and still very much in shock. Olympia was pleased to see that Becci McClain and Ellen Brody were seated among them.

Thelma, as the moderator, called the impromptu meeting to order and asked Pastor Olympia if she would please say a prayer. When she concluded the prayer and while she still had their attention, Olympia went on to say that she was not there as decision maker, because she had no history with them. She was there as a minister, to offer support and comfort and the benefit of her own decision-making experience, if asked.

"I came today because I care about you, and I want to be with you in a time of crisis. I am with you today as a listener and an advisor, if called upon, and in addition to that, I'll make the coffee."

This produced a few wan smiles around the room.

Michael Nee began the conversation. "We all know we will need to get the full reports before we make any decisions. We still don't know how bad the damage is and what we're covered for. I do know for a fact that we increased our building insurance a few years ago. But we will deal with the numbers at the next meeting. Right now all we can really do is hang in there, do the best we can to keep the congregation informed, which, considering how many don't use email, is going to mean a lot of phone calling. So we can't really do very much right now. Still, I thought it was important for us all to be together and have a time to say what's on our minds."

Becci leaned over and whispered into Olympia's ear "How long have you got?"

"Have you decided if you are going to accept the rabbi's offer?" asked Olympia.

"I thought you weren't here to offer advice, Pastor."

Olympia didn't miss the jab, nor did she miss a beat. "Not advice, Michael, more like a question about logistics. As the preacher in the pulpit, I need to know if you are going to continue holding services, and if so, where? It's a reasonable question. There's an argument for taking a week or two off to collect yourselves and just as strong an argument for getting right back on the horse and keeping on."

"Sorry, it's been a long day. We're all a little touchy."

"Of course you are. We all are," said Olympia.

In the end there was general agreement to accept the rabbi's offer and to continue with a regular schedule of services. They would defer any further discussion of building repair/restoration/demolition until the figures were in.

Becci raised her hand. "I can work from home. Everything's on the computer, and I think the offices weren't damaged. I can go back there and get out what I need."

Well, there's damn sure nothing left worth retrieving in my office now that

you've all done such a thorough cleaning, thought Olympia. "That's great, Becci," she said. "I can work from home as well. I have a full office set up there. I even have a copier and a fax machine. We can set up a couple of group Skype chat rooms, and you all can have regular meetings and patch me in when you want. Who knows, there might even be a spare room we can use for small meetings and office space in the synagogue building. We can certainly ask."

They were interrupted by an insistent cell phone ring tone.

Nee took the call and then reported the message. "Constance and Ted have finished up at the church and are on their way over here. The disaster people have secured it and made sure the police will keep an eye on it.

They think we should have some figures by Tuesday. So I guess that's when we'll have our next meeting." He paused. "Um, do you think you could come, Pastor?"

"Of course I can. Thank you for including me."

Olympia silently noted that nothing in their future plans and strategies included anything to do with the secret life of David Cameron.

CHAPTER 34

While Olympia was dealing with the affairs of the church, literally and figuratively, Frederick was standing, shovel in hand, in the back garden. By now, with some sage advice from the home and garden people, some cautionary advice from his good lady wife and a realistic look at the budget allotment for his latest undertaking, he was mapping out a design for how to get the water that would fall from the roof and run through the gutters and down the spouts into holding barrels that would be affixed to sunken hoses with turn-off valves, which would direct the water into his pond and adjacent waterfall. This wonderful, free water would be then elevated by a hidden pump and carried up through the back of the rocks that formed the waterfall. On command it would trickle merrily down to the pond declivity, where it would bubble around for a while before starting the cycle all over again—all at the click of a remote wand.

This last, the availability of a remote electronic control device, he'd carefully kept from Olympia. He was determined that some part of this should be a surprise for her. Imagine the delight at being able to click on or off your own personal waterfall, not to mention the imbedded color-changing lights also independently operated, from the comfort of a bug-proof conservatory. Frederick loved the wonders of electronics and what they offered, even if they did confuse him sometimes. But this time, he'd asked advice and followed it. No more domestic disasters. Still, the issue of how best to route the hoses from the gutters to the holding tanks and from the holding tanks to the reservoir behind the rock wall remained a problem. It was basically a matter of gravity. That much he understood. The rocky, sandy and clay pitted geology and geography of New England, not so much.

But Frederick was determined. He would have his beautiful, visually soothing, energy- and water-saving network of connecting hoses, and his beloved would have a backlit waterfall. Along with all this wonder they both would have beautiful tame koi to feed and watch. The digging was scheduled to begin tomorrow.

The unmistakable sound of a VW bus engine sputtering up the drive pulled him from his aquatic and piscine meanderings. "What ho, my love?"

"Cautious forward progress on one front and dead silence on the other is probably the best description I can come up with. They still need hard money facts. Amount of damage, costs of repair versus total knock-down and rebuild, endowment issues, and profound grief and shock over the building … and the whole time, not a word about Cameron." She shook her head. "I feel so badly for them, it's like they've stepped on a landmine, been hit with an earthquake and flattened by a tornado in the space of forty-eight hours. They simply don't know what's hit them. I'll do what I can, if they'll let me."

She dropped her tote bag on the ground and collapsed into a lawn chair. "It certainly puts the clergy misconduct on the back burner at the moment. Trouble is, I'm afraid some of them, at least, will try and use this as a way to drop the whole thing and gallop right past it. You know, pretend it never happened. All I know is that there's a lot in play over there. It's one hell of a tangle, and they have no idea which string they should pick out and unwind first."

She shook her head. "And if they can pick it apart and get to the middle, what then? I have a very bad feeling about this, Frederick. I think it's going to get considerably worse before, or even if, it can ever get better."

Frederick walked to his wife's side and took her hand. "I never thought I'd ever say this, my love, but might you have bitten off more than you can chew? Are you in over your head? I don't want you to become collateral damage here."

"You mean, when all else fails, blame the newcomer? If I hadn't opened that ugly door, none of this would have happened? It all went downhill after the new minister arrived?"

"Something like that."

"Let's just put it this way: I'm not going to walk away

right now. But if it becomes apparent that my staying will only prolong the agony, or worse, that I become the target for all their rage and anger, then of course I'll withdraw. I don't have an actual contract with them yet. We were going to do that at the next meeting. As it stands right now I am there because we all agreed I would stay on for the time being. So I guess that's where I stand. Yes for now, and don't forget to watch my own back.

"I'm not going to let the sex-abuse thing drop. I have an ethical and professional commitment to that. The women that he victimized will need help to get on with their lives. They need to have their pain validated and acknowledged. It's become a separate issue—interconnected, to be sure, but still separate. This I can do."

Frederick kissed her hand and released it. "Glass of wine, my love?"

"A big one, please, but first, why don't you take me around the back garden and tell me how the pond plans are progressing?"

CHAPTER 35

The next scheduled meeting of the full board was scheduled for some time in the very near future, but the power core of Thelma, Selma, Mike Nee, and Ted Jennings called another secret meeting on Monday afternoon to plan, control and orchestrate the agenda of the full meeting. Power is as power does, and the church, their church, was in crisis. Whereas a fire could happen to anybody, and insurance covered such things, the issue of the predator pastor was theirs alone. Essentially they were in fight-or-flight mode for themselves individually and for the future of the church they'd called home for generations.

They'd eventually come to the uncomfortable agreement that there was no walking away from the irrefutable evidence of David Cameron's misconduct. Along with that was the uncomfortable reality that through their collective denial and silence over the years, they had in one way or another tacitly condoned what had happened. Like Adam and Eve caught naked in the garden, they knew what they'd done, and they were sore afraid. More than that, they were deeply ashamed.

Nee was the first to speak "I hate to say this, but there's a part of me that wishes the whole thing had burned to the ground. That way we'd be totally done with it, and we'd have to start all over again, you know, wipe the slate clean of everything. As it is right now, we're stuck trying to figure out what to do with the wreckage."

Ted held up his hand. "Remember, we still haven't decided whether to wreck or reconstruct. We can't do that until we get the final figures. And that's just the building. There's another issue on the table, and we all know it. Frankly, I think it's bigger than a burned building."

"Not so," said Thelma. "We, or rather the whole board, can make the building decision any time we want to. We will get the insurance money, and we have the endowment. Between the two, we can pretty much do what we want, and that's why we're here right now, to decide what that is going to be."

Nee shook his head and crossed his arms. "Correction. We could always do what we wanted, and look where it's gotten us. I think it's time we take a look at the bigger picture here and that is, what are we going to rebuild? We have a very embarrassing and shameful elephant in the room named David Cameron. I don't think we can start rebuilding anything until we deal with that."

Ted waved his hand. "Pastor Olympia told us she

knows about people who are trained in this sort of thing. I don't know about you two, but I'm ready to call in the heavy artillery. I'm over my head, out of my league, and I don't mind saying I need help."

"Second the motion," said Thelma.

"In favor," added her sister.

"I suggest we call a meeting of the full board as soon as we have the facts and figures regarding the damage and repair, and then with everyone present, we put every-thing else on the table. And I mean everything."

"Should it be a closed meeting, or do you want to invite Pastor Olympia?" asked Selma.

Ted gave them all a hard look. "There's no question but she should be there. She knows what's happened. She has a clear head, and don't ask me why, but I trust her."

"I think we can all agree she's not in it for the money."

"I don't know. Look at that scrap heap of a car she drives. Maybe she wants to get a new car."

The little joke at Olympia's expense was the healing glimmer of light under the door they all needed to see. Maybe there would be a way around all this, but there was only one place to begin, and that was at the bottom, because from there the only way out was up.

CHAPTER 36

"Hello, this is Gloria. Thank you for calling The Birchwood retirement and assisted living Community. How may I direct your call?" OMG, thought Olympia, a real person just answered the phone. Be still my heart.

"Good morning. This is Reverend Olympia Brown speaking. I'm the new minister at a church that one of your residents, David Cameron, used to pastor. There's a few of us here who would like to come out and say hello to him. Is he receiving visitors?"

"Oh, good heavens yes. He's here and he just loves to have company." She added *sotto voce*, "They all do. When might you be coming?"

"TBA," said Olympia convincingly. "I had to find out if he'd actually know us and if it would mean anything. I heard it was a pretty massive stroke." Olympia was pushing the patient privacy boundaries, and she knew it.

"Well, he is almost totally disabled, but inside he's still

as bright as a button. That part's sad, I guess. But he's happy enough here. He loves the attention we give him."

"Say, what's his room number? I'll bet there are a few people who would like to send him a card from the church."

Olympia could hear the smile in the woman's voice. "Oh, they all love to get mail. It'll make his day. It's 265 in the Evergreen Unit. We name all of our units after trees. It sounds more uplifting than words like north or south."

"Well then, Gloria, I'll call and let you know if and when we can get it together." I'm going to make his day, all right, thought Olympia, but I'm not going to do it with a dollar store get well card. She smiled back into the phone.

"You do that, Reverend, and thank you for calling The Birchwood. Is there anything else I can help you with?

The woman was back on script. Olympia wrote down the room number and filed the information in the folder labeled "Use when needed, and take as directed."

CHAPTER 37

On Tuesday morning Olympia got a call from Ellen Brody, who said that she'd spoken to the woman she'd made reference to in the meeting on Saturday, and yes, she was willing to meet with Olympia as long as Ellen was there. "No promises after that, but she did agree to one meeting."

"What's her name?" asked Olympia.

"Carol Johnson."

"I owe you, Ellen."

"No, you don't."

Olympia disconnected the call and was making a note to self to call Jim when the phone rang for a second time.

"Pastor Olympia? This is Grace Foster. You called me last week. I'm the woman who cut you short and hung up on you last week. I owe you an apology. I've thought it over and decided that I would like to talk to you."

Olympia fired off a quick prayer for guidance.

"Grace, thank you so much for calling me back. You may or may not know this, but there's been a fire in the church ..."

"That's probably what gave me the courage to call you, Pastor. I saw it on the news and figured the fire might help close that chapter for me, but it was just the opposite. It brought everything back. I'm having nightmares. Maybe it's a sign from God. Either way, I'm willing."

"I have a private office in my home where we can talk, or I can come to your house. A coffee shop or restaurant is way too public, and this is far too personal for a telephone conversation. Maybe a park or a green space somewhere with benches?"

"Actually, lots of supermarkets have coffee shops now. There's one that's about halfway between us. I checked it out on Google Maps. A grocery store is about as impersonal as it gets, wouldn't you say? I'd suggest mid-morning, after the breakfast crowd is out and before the lunch crowd hits, or the in-between time in the afternoon, when all the babies are napping and the kids are coming home from school. It's hardly a destination eatery, but it is a relatively anonymous convenience."

"If that works for you, it works for me. When are you available?"

"How about this afternoon? The sooner the better, like before I chicken out." A short laugh.

"Two-thirty?"

"Perfect."

"How will I know you?"

"I'll know you; I Google-d you and found a picture. I'll be there early, and I'll wave when you come in."

Of course, Google image search, thought Olympia, how could I have possibly forgotten?

"I'll be on time."

"Thank you, Pastor." Her words were barely audible.

Olympia powered up her computer and fired off a quick email to Ellen Brody. "We may have lift-off. I just heard from a victim I tried to contact last week. I'm meeting her this afternoon. I will get back to you after that."

CHAPTER 38

Grace Foster waved at Olympia as she entered the Coffee Korner. She was a smallish woman with dark curly hair and a bright collection of bangle bracelets on the arm she lifted in greeting. The coffee and sitting area was just to the right of the main entrance of The Market Place. It was one of those giant new, all-in-one supermarket/pharmacy/bank/shoe repair and florist shop complexes with parking for what looked like thousands. The woman was predictably seated at a back corner table. Across the room in the other far corner Olympia could see the doors to the restrooms.

The decor was neutral, beige and brown and scratch-proof, transient in the choice of self-serve everything out of machines and noisy enough to be completely private. It was pleasant enough for a quick cup but not a place where you would linger.

Surprisingly, however, the cappuccino Olympia purchased from the coffee machine was delicious. She carried it, hot and steaming, toward the table and sat down opposite Grace.

"Thank you for coming, Pastor."

"No, Grace, thank you for your courage in stepping forward. I'm sure you know the statistics. For every woman who dares speak up, there are hundreds who don't. It's just too risky. But I promise you my absolute confidence. Nothing, not one word of what you say to me, will go past the edges of this table."

Grace stared down into her own coffee for a few moments before beginning her story. "I started going to South River right after my divorce. I was looking for a place for the kids and for me, too, I guess. You know what happens after you get a divorce. People take sides, and your married friends drop you like a rock. I was lonely."

Olympia nodded.

"Anyway, within weeks Cameron was grooming me. Of course I didn't know that's what it was called. All I know is that I thought I'd died and gone to heaven. Here's this gorgeous, charismatic man that everyone loves and looks up to, and he's not married, and he's coming on to me. Behind closed doors, of course. Our precious little secret."

Not wanting to interrupt her story, Olympia said nothing.

"And it was consensual. Boy was it ever. No one could ever say he forced me. I would have followed him to the moon and back. And then boom, it was over, but not before he took the pictures."

Olympia nodded in mute understanding.

"He gave me a story about not wanting to get too involved, that God and the church were his true calling, but his love for me was so great he was starting to question his vocation and, much as he didn't want to, he had to end it. Then I started calling him. That's when he told me about the pictures. I couldn't believe what I was hearing. He had me." She paused, not bothering to fight back the tears. "I dropped out of his life, and my stupidity haunts me to this day."

Olympia reached for the woman's hand. "You weren't stupid, Grace, you were a victim, and you still are. This was not your fault. Men like him know exactly what they're doing, and they don't care about who they go after. He was a serial predator. You were likely neither the first nor the last of the women whose lives he's destroyed."

She paused for a calming breath. "I have a personal loathing for people in power, ministers particularly, who abuse a position of sacred trust to denigrate and victimize people who turn to them for help and guidance. So much so that I've made it a personal mission to seek out victims of these monsters and help them find peace."

Grace looked Olympia straight in the eye. "Will you help me?"

"Absolutely, I will help you."

Olympia told Grace what had happened to Cameron, where he was now and outlined a still nascent plan to confront him. After that she asked Grace if she would be willing to meet with some of the other victims.

No hesitation. "Yes."

"It won't be easy, but we'll take it one day at a time. The plan is still in the development stages, I say the sooner the better."

"Totally," said Grace.

CHAPTER 39

On Wednesday, seated in a high-backed booth in the agreed upon Panera, Betty Almasi told Olympia a story disturbingly similar to the one she'd heard the day before. The only difference was that Betty had still been married when she and her husband approached Pastor Cameron for couples counseling. It wasn't long before Cameron recommended separate counseling sessions, saying it was important for each of them to speak his or her mind without the other present. And so it went. Then, when he was ready to move on, the pictures and the threats.

"You can't imagine the guilt I felt. The marriage fell apart, and I blamed myself totally. I never told anyone until now. That man is totally evil. Not just bad, Reverend Brown, evil. Devil spawn."

When Betty had talked herself out, Olympia comforted her and explained how she was not a sinner, she was a victim, one who had been expertly targeted by a vicious serial predator.

Finally, Olympia told her she was working on a plan that might bring some closure to her and the others, and to that end, would she be willing to meet with the other victims and hear what it was?

I've carried this way, way, way too long." She was rubbing her forehead. "Just tell me when and where. I'm in."

CHAPTER 40

B ecause there was no space in the church for Olympia to have a private meeting, Olympia invited Ellen Brody and Carol Johnson to come to her home in Brookfields. The two women arrived together, Carol with flowers and Ellen cradling a white bakery box that could only be something sweet. Olympia was certain she could actually smell the sugar when they entered the kitchen.

After the preliminary niceties and courteous questions about the age and history of the house, the three women carried their iced tea and their pastries into the office. Once there, they settled themselves into a semicircle around the antique chest that served as both guest blanket storage and coffee table.

Olympia opened the conversation by thanking Carol for coming and assuring her that anything she said would be held in pastoral confidence. She alone would determine if anything went beyond the space they occupied. Now she spoke softly.

"What would you like me to know about what happened between you and David Cameron?"

Carol looked down at her restless hands. "I could go on for hours, but the short form is, I first started coming to the church after my husband died, and I was left alone with two little kids. I was looking for comfort and community, and he was standing at the door waiting for me. I mean, I walked right into it. There he was, handsome as they come, single and in need of comfort himself. He wasted no time in telling me that I had to be a gift directly from God. Were we not supposed to comfort those who grieve? He comforted me all right. Within the week he was calling me to see how I was doing, suggesting we go for a walk, that the exercise and fresh air would do me good, and even helping me find babysitters from the church youth group. I thought I'd died and gone to heaven. In a matter of two weeks I went from a stunned, grieving widow to an insanely infatuated, head-over-heals in love crazy lady and the next in the line of succession, or so I now understand. I loved the attention, thrived on the secrecy and the mystery and the forbidden intrigue, the secret phone signals, even the sleazy motels. God, I can still smell the bleach." She shook her head and wiped her eyes. "And then it all fell apart."

"What happened?" whispered Olympia.

"Of course I wanted to marry him, and from the day I first mentioned it, he started pulling back, but not before he took the pictures. He said he wanted them so he could think about me when we were apart. Jesus, how could I have been so stupid?"

"I can't begin to imagine the pain you have been carrying all these years."

"Pain and shame and then helpless, impotent rage, because he had me. That's when he announced that we needed to separate. He told me his love for me was so great that it was beginning to affect his ministry to others. God would never want that, so we had to sacrifice our love for the greater good of the church … and oh, by the way, I have these pictures, and if you ever so much as breathe a word to anyone, I'll say you sent them to me." Carol was shouting and sobbing openly now, the restless hands now clenched into fists she was pounding on her knees.

Olympia reached for one of Carol's hands, and Ellen took the other, and for a while the three sat in mute and agonizing witness to the woman's naked pain. But now it was out, and they believed her, and she knew they believed her.

When the sobs and the shaking subsided, Carol raised her eyes. Olympia squeezed her hand and said, "We have heard you. We are witness to your pain. And now, if you don't mind, I suggest we three just sit with all of this for a little bit."

In time, Olympia asked Carol if she would be willing to meet with the other victims and then all of them together go and stand before David Cameron, date and time to be mutually agreed upon.

She flinched. "I'll have to think about that. Let me

know where and when, and by then I should have an answer for you."

"Would you believe I still have a sermon to write and a service to prepare for? Right now we are holding our services at the local synagogue until we decide what the future of the congregation is going to be."

CHAPTER 41

On Saturday morning, despite the fact that she still had a sermon to write, Olympia decided take a drive over to the church and look at the damage for herself with no one asking questions or offering a running commentary. She had a key, if one was needed, and while there, she could collect the few personal things she'd left in the office. She'd written more than one sermon while sitting behind the wheel and dictating it into her phone. Driving alone was powerful thinking and problem-solving time.

"Do you want me to come along with you?" asked Frederick.

"I don't think so, love. It's not going to be much more than a drive-by. I just want to see it for myself and by myself."

The two were companionably finishing breakfast. The day ahead was predicted to be a mix of scattered

showers and periods of humid sunshine. Her mother
would call it thunderstorm weather.

"Don't forget your brolly."

"I keep one in the car. Better safe than sorry—or in
this case, wet."

"Ta-ra, pet. Do you know how long you'll be?"

"As long as it takes, I guess, probably most of the
morning. I might as well do some errands while I'm out.
Let's say I'll be back in the early to mid- afternoon."

"Righty-oh, then," said her husband. He was a man
with a plan. The earth movers were coming today, and it
appeared that for once fortune had smiled upon him. His
lady wife with her strong opinions, much as he loved her,
would be otherwise and elsewhere occupied, and he
would have the final say on the size, scope and location
of the excavation. Frederick was a happy man.

BY THE TIME OLYMPIA REACHED THE RUINED CHURCH,
she'd already been through two brief downpours, a flash
of brilliant sunshine and a double rainbow. She accepted
this last as a sign of divine blessing and secular good luck
as she walked across the empty parking lot toward the
door that led to the relatively undamaged end of the
building. The smell of burnt wet wood hung heavily in
air, and the wet pavement from the recent shower only
served to reflect and intensify it. She wrinkled her nose.

The fluttering yellow tape that surrounded the place
warned passersby of danger, no entry and to keep out,
but that was intended for vandals and looters and morbid
curiosity seekers. She was the pastor. She had a right to

cross the line, and she was not so stupid as to try and climb around the rubble on her own. She did, however, want to have a good look at the damage without someone watching and taking notes. She pulled her phone out of her pocket and opened the camera app, then continued around the remains of the building until she came to the burned-out wall. What she found literally took her breath away. The damage was far greater than she'd imagined. The entire wall and most of the roof above it were gone, everything inside charred and water soaked. The pulpit that she'd vacated a week ago was now hanging at a crazy angle, and the hymnbooks were open, soaked and scattered, looking for all the world like dead and wounded birds flapping useless wings. There was no need to record this.

She pocketed her phone, completed her walk-around of the ruin and let herself into the still intact part of the building that housed the social hall, the formal parlor, the kitchen and the offices. The place was dead quiet, and the smell was overpowering, but the structure was sound, and there was nothing to trip over or fall through. Olympia made her way to the pastor's study but stopped when she heard something—or thought she did. A fluttering scraping sound. A whimper. An animal? A skunk or raccoon that had come in through the burned-out area looking for food? A trapped bird? A looter?

Her first thought was concern for the animal; the second and far more practical one was concern for herself. Trapped, scared animals can attack. Be sensible. No quick moves. Be very quiet.

She paused outside the kitchen door, took a deep

breath and then began pounding on the door with both fists. This would scare whatever it was into hiding or escape, and she would have a chance to peek inside. In the silence that followed her volley, she slowly opened the door.

"Just leave me alone." Ted, the treasurer, was cowering in the far corner of the kitchen. "Pastor! No. Just go away." He covered his face with his hands.

Olympia stood her ground. "I'm not going anywhere, Ted. You need help."

"Get out," he screamed. "You started it all. Just get out and leave me alone, I'm begging you." Then he collapsed onto the floor, howling like a wounded animal.

Olympia ran to him and shouted. "I'm going to call 911." She pulled out her phone but he grabbed her hand.

"No-no, please, not that. I'm okay."

"You are anything but okay, but if you'll talk to me, I won't call 911—if you don't, I will."

"Help me up."

She reached out her hand and helped to ease the broken man into a marginally upright position.

"Come on, then. My office probably stinks, but I think I can open a window, and I think there are still two chairs in there."

She put her arm around him and guided him out of the kitchen and into the study where she lowered him onto the nearest chair.

"Tell me what you were doing in there, Ted."

"I did it."

"You did what?"

"I started the fire."

"You what?"

He nodded miserably. The distraught man was slowly coming back into his body and finding his voice. "It's a long story, Pastor."

"I'm not going anywhere. You can tell me about it, if you want to. I am bound by the vows of my ordination and my own moral code to keep your confidence."

He waited for a few more moments and then began the story of how he'd withdrawn and used almost half of the endowment fund. It started innocently at first. He needed money for a mortgage payment and would of course put it right back. But before long one payment became three and then five and then ten. He always intended to put it back, but since no one ever wanted to touch the endowment, he thought his secret was safe. He was the treasurer and would remain so until he could make things right. And by God, he would.

Then the board started discussing an improvement initiative. The old building needed new wiring throughout, plumbing upgrades, insulation, roof repairs. It had all been neglected for so long. He knew that if they went into the endowment for the money, they would find out what he'd done. However, if they had a damaging event, a tornado, a tree falling on the building or … a fire, then the insurance would cover everything. The endowment and his secret would be safe, and he would be able to get the money back before anybody learned of what he'd done. With his plan in place, he picked the day and started the fire by cramming a penny in the fuse box and overloading all the circuits.

"Why on earth did you choose a Sunday?" asked Olympia.

"Attendance is lower in the summer. There's no snow to get in the way of the fire trucks or freeze people when they ran out of the building, and who would start a fire when he himself was in the building? No one would ever suspect me. I had the perfect alibi. I was in plain sight the whole time. I knew that it would start in the wiring and that we had good smoke alarms and plenty of exits. I had a plan, and I was good to go, and ..." he paused.

"Until what?"

"Until you came and told us about the photographs."

"I don't understand. What does that have to do with the endowment?"

His voice was getting stronger now. He rubbed his eyes. "I knew about Pastor Cameron. I didn't know about the pictures, but several of us knew or strongly suspected what he was up to, and we looked the other way. He was good for business. The numbers were growing. He was a presence in town, and even more than that, we didn't want to bring shame on the church. Old families and all that crap. What the hell was I thinking? Between that and what I did with the endowment, I've turned my back on everything I thought I believed in. Believe it or not, I thought maybe this way I could atone for what I'd done."

"So what were you doing here today?"

"Call me a prodigal son, if you want, but I wanted to come back here today to put it all right. I've changed my will and left the money from the sale of my house to the church. Then I explained it all, I mean everything, in a letter and left a copy in my desk at home and mailed another one to you. I came back here to put an end to it."

"You mean …"

He nodded. "I have a loaded gun in my pocket."

Olympia held out her hand. "May I have it?"

He flinched and stepped back. "What are you going to do?"

"I promised you my confidence, and you have it. I'm not going to do anything without your permission. I am going to ask you to give me the gun and then I would like to take you to the nearest hospital and get you to a doctor who can help you. This is not worth dying for."

The tension in the room was breath stopping. Olympia waited, praying for strength and guidance.

"What if I do go to a doctor? What then?"

Olympia exhaled. "You will be safe, and you will get the help you need, and I think I might have an idea about the money. But first things first. Will you come with me?" She held out her hand. Ted, now pale and shaking, reached for her outstretched hand and unsteadily pulled himself out of the chair to his feet.

"What are we going to tell people when I don't show up tomorrow?"

"I'll tell them the truth, just maybe not all of it. When I get home I'll call the members of the board and tell them that I came in and found you on the floor and called 911. When we got you to the hospital, they decided to keep you there for observation. Cards welcome, but no visits please. That should take care of it."

Olympia held out her other hand. "Now that you're up, may I please have the gun?"

OLYMPIA DIDN'T RETURN HOME UNTIL MUCH LATER that afternoon. When she did pull in, the designated earth had been moved, the hole had been dug, the black plastic was in place and Frederick, sweating like a pig, was cheerfully lumping rocks from point A to point B.

"How was your day?" he called out, smiling over the rubble.

"Quiet as a crypt and twice as interesting." she gave him a wry smile. "How long have you got? I just need to make a phone call, and then I'll join you in the glass of wine you were just about to pour for me."

August 1867

It has taken me some time to find a few moments to return to these most precious and private pages. The storm that I spoke of in my previous entry was the stuff of legend. We lost two large trees. The larger of the two fell just feet from the kitchen door, but the smaller one is still resting on the roof of the barn. I am grateful for Susan's husband Charles and my dear Richard. The two have been working like proper lumbermen taking it all to pieces. We shall not lack for firewood this winter, hard, slow burning oak, and we still have much in excess to give to those in need. Much of the town is still badly damaged, but thanks be to God, no lives were lost.

And now for the good news. After the visit with Olympia Brown, the entire congregation gathered in the church proper to consider my proposal to open a school for girls and young women and ask for the endorsement and sponsorship (not money mind you) of the church. There was much heated and sometimes incendiary discussion on the matter, but the turning point came when Reverend Meacham offered the gardener's cottage on his own land for our use.

The man is loved and respected by all, and if he can give us not only his full throated support but a location on his own property, there were none left to stand against it. There is much ahead of us, but we have taken the first step. And yet, there is still one stone left in all of this that remains unturned, the wicked whispering about Susan and me.

More anon, LFW

CHAPTER 42

It was a warm, drowsy kind of afternoon, and David Cameron was slumped in a light doze when Angela Hendryx knocked and then entered to bring him down to the community room for the afternoon social hour. Tea and glasses of wine were on offer along with light snacks and ready help with eating and drinking, if needed. The wine was a recent addition to the daily offerings, and considering how eagerly the residents looked forward to it, it was now a regular feature on the daily schedule.

When Cameron didn't respond to her knock, Angela moved closer and started to say his name when a flickering image on his ever-present tablet caught her attention and stopped her mid-stride. She stifled a squawk of dismay and disgust at what she was looking at. Pastor Cameron had found himself an adult movie site and had fallen asleep part way through the action.

Without making a sound she tapped the off button and spoke his name. "David?"

He opened his eyes and with obvious difficulty focused on the woman standing by his chair. Then his eyes widened and shifted to the tablet next to his right arm.

"It's still there, David. Nobody's taken it. You must have turned it off and fallen asleep. Would you like to come down for a cup of tea?"

He responded with an almost imperceptible shake of his head. No.

"A glass of wine, then?"

This time, he opened his eyes wider, made a grunting sound and tried to work his lopsided mouth into a smile.

"I'll take that for a yes. Come on, then, let's have a look at you. "

She went into the bathroom and came out with a wet face cloth and a comb and set about smoothing down his hair and wiping his face and hands.

"There now. Bright as a new penny, twice as handsome and not a minute late. Let's go." She grabbed the handles of his chair, spun him around and then stopped.

"Say, would you like me to take the tablet off your chair and put it on your bed table? No sense having it in the way when you're trying to have a drink now, is there?"

A vague nod. He was clearly tired. Life was such hard work for him now. Angela detached the tablet and left it on his nightstand. "I'll hook it up when we get you back after dinner. Is that okay?" Another labored nod. "Come on then, you, it's party time." The woman was professionally and relentlessly cheery.

When she'd delivered David to the common room and parked him near the wine and snacks table, she handed the feeding and drinking duty over to one of the volunteers, saying she needed to run to the bathroom and would be right back. But the bathroom was not on the itinerary. Angela went back to her locker and grabbed the tube of super glue she kept for emergency quick fixes. There were times when a work order, sent through the proper channels, could take up to a week to get done, and a quick squirt of super glue could have things in working order in minutes—or in this case, exactly the opposite.

With the glue in her pocket, she slipped into David's room, shut the door behind her and headed directly for the nightstand and the tablet. One quick well aimed squeeze of glue in the USB port and a swipe of the face cloth she'd just used to clean his face to remove any remaining traces of glue around the port and she was done.

Minutes later she was back in the community room, chatting with the residents, wiping chins, and stroking trembling hands. Angela was very good at what she did. She put her whole heart and soul into her work with these people. She honestly loved and respected them, and even if they couldn't say it or show it, it was clear they knew it.

And tonight, or maybe not until tomorrow, when they told her that David's tablet had stopped working and asked whatever were they going to do, it was his right hand, she would say, "Oh I'll have a look at it. I'm pretty good with electronics. These things happen. It's not the end of the world."

LATER THAT EVENING ANGELA WAS SITTING IN THE kitchen with her open Bible in front of her and a glass of iced tea next to her elbow. She was troubled about what she'd done that day and was now checking to see if there was a commandment that dealt specifically with or prohibited messing with or disabling thy neighbor's electronic devices. But nothing in the basic ten came even close. She was not coveting, bearing false witness, adulterating, dishonoring her parents … no, she was good in that department.

Still, the troubling thoughts persisted until the comforting words of "The Lord's Prayer" came to her. "Forgive us our trespasses as we forgive those who trespass against us," and even more affirming, "Lead us not into temptation, but deliver me from evil." There it was. Problem solved. She was comforted knowing she was leading what once must have been a good man away from the ways of evil and temptation. She knew she would be forgiven, because she would of course forgive him were the circumstances reversed. Of course she would.

Thus assured, she drained the remains of the iced tea and made a personal decision to raid the cookie jar before checking to see what was on TV that evening.

CHAPTER 43

At home in their overstuffed Victorian home, Selma and Thelma were upset and irritable. To say they were unsettled would be an understatement. Considering they were twins, a more accurate description might be to say they were doubly beside themselves and couldn't say whether they were coming or going. The two women had invested their entire lives in the South River Community Church. At first they were the adorable twin baby girls baptized as infants, children whom everyone loved and helped to raise. They'd never married, preferring the familiarity of each other's company to separation and the interference of a stranger in their ordered lives. Their early lives centered on the church, and as they grew into adulthood, their parallel business careers provided enough money for them to be substantial donors to the church and enthusiastic supporters of its many activities. Now, as retired ladies, their time revolved around the social activity cycle of the church year. They were the official caterers, greeters, gardeners, oral historians and self-appointed comforters of those in need. They were also the unquestioned authority on how things should and should not be done, and no one in his right mind ever dared suggest otherwise.

But that was then, and this was now. The church they'd built their life around was in partial ruin, and everything they thought they held sacred about that church was about to be smeared with the most disgusting and embarrassing scandal. The ground had shifted beneath their sensibly shod feet, and the two ladies were anchorless in a shifting tide of events over which, for once in their lifelong togetherness, they had absolutely no control. Sherry was not enough to deal with this. The ladies had ordered a take-out delivery for their dinner and were now sipping steadily from two oversized tumblers of very old, very expensive scotch.

"We didn't want to know, did we, Selma? We'd both heard the rumors and the gossip, but we turned a deaf ear, didn't we? I feel that makes us part of what happened to those poor women. What's that word they use nowadays? Enabling?" She grimaced and shook her head. "I feel so ashamed."

"I don't know what I feel right now," Selma mused. "I know I'm mad as a wet hen for being played the fool, and at the same time I'm sick about what happened and terrified about what's going to come out in the media. And mark my words, dear sister, it absolutely will.

Watching the mighty fall is the stuff the bottom feeders just love.

"I'm afraid of what people will say about us as a church and a congregation," she continued. We've been watching this kind of thing play out with the Catholics, and haven't we been the smug ones through it all, pointing fingers anywhere but at ourselves." She made a face of disgust. "I'm so mad I could just spit. I wanted to think we were better than this."

"We were," said Thelma, raising her glass toward her sister, "and I believe we can be again. I don't know what that looks like right now. We'll have a better idea after the big meeting next Sunday, but I'll tell you one thing, I'm not going to put aside everything I've invested in and just walk away. It could be that the handwriting's been on the wall for some time now, but we refused to see it. I believe everything happens for a reason, even this."

"You would say that, and you always did. Can't say I always loved you for it, Miss Pollyanna Goody-Two-Shoes, but you are what you are, and I'm stuck with you."

"I'm the optimist and you're...." Thelma held up her pointer finger, "the realist!"

The two women, aided by the amount and superiority of the scotch, were warming to their gentle ripostes when the three-note door chime interrupted their lubricated flow of words. Selma covered her lips and stifled a modest burp. "We are saved from any further unpleasant familial discourse by the bell. I do believe our dinner has arrived," she observed.

"I'll get the wine and you get the door, Selma or Scarlett or whatever you say your name is, because I do give a damn, my dear, and even if tomorrow is another day, I'm hungry now!"

CHAPTER 44

On Sunday Olympia and the rabbi stood side by side at the front door of the synagogue and welcomed the cautious, curious and battle-weary members of the South River congregation. Many had never been inside a Jewish house of worship and were trying not to look as out of place as they felt. Slowly they trickled in and took seats in pews that looked remarkably like the pews in their own church. The men accepted the yarmulkes that were offered to them as well as neighborly help in putting them in place.

Any lingering feelings of awkwardness or discomfort were soon dispelled when the rabbi and the president of the congregation walked up to the *bema*, the pulpit, and held out their arms in welcome to Olympia and the other people sitting before them. They sang out, *"Hineh ma tov uma na'im, Shevet achim gam yachad,"* which translated to, "How good and pleasant it is for brothers and sisters to sit together."

After the service the women of the congregation hosted a kosher coffee hour and later explained to anyone who was interested the rules and practices of keeping a kosher kitchen. It was suggested that maybe, when things quieted down for everyone, they could plan a shared potluck dinner.

Olympia stood off to the side, drinking some really good coffee and watching it all. Her people were standing around eating sweets, drinking coffee lightened with artificial creamer, *schmoozing*, a good Jewish word befitting the occasion, and having a good time together. To the untrained eye things looked almost normal, and Olympia allowed herself a very small and very quiet sigh of contentment. We can do this, she thought, and if not, we'll damn sure try. She was already looking forward to the following Sunday when it all wouldn't feel so new, and they began to settle into their new home in the community.

Meanwhile she had more than enough work to do in the days to come, much of which she couldn't discuss with anyone.

CHAPTER 45

On Monday, despite the fact that she was emotionally wrung out with all that was happening around her, Olympia was daring to feel moderately hopeful as she finished up the breakfast dishes. South River had a place to hold services. As much as they didn't want to, they had at least acknowledged there was problem with Pastor David. She'd now had conversations with three victims, and she had Ellen's support on the congregational side of her efforts. Her next challenge would be to arrange a day and a time to pay a surprise visit to David Edward Cameron. Maybe some of this unholy mess was starting to come together.

And then what, Olympia? She didn't have a ready answer for that other than take it one day, one crisis, at a time.

The cats heard the tentative knock at the back door before Olympia did. The second, more insistent one got her attention, and she went to see who was there. It was Rayna, both arms around a hefty box, no hat, no dog.

"Rayna, what in the world brings you to my back door?" She did not ask how she'd found her way there, where the dog was or anything else that might have indicated or clarified the intent of her presence. "Do come in and sit down, and I'll get us both something cool to drink."

"I hope I'm not interrupting you, Pastor. I deliberately didn't call you first, because if I had, I might not have come."

Frederick was out, and Olympia was alone. Under other circumstances Olympia would have gently but firmly turned the woman away, offered to drive her home or, at the very least, taken her to a coffee shop for a chat. But she didn't.

"It goes without saying that I wasn't expecting you, but Frederick is out, so we have the place to ourselves, and I do have time to see you. Would you like to go into my office or stay right here in the kitchen with the cats?"

"You know me, I'm an animal lover. I vote for right here. It's so bright and sunny. Kitchens are the heart of the home, don't you think?"

Rayna set the unopened box at one end of the kitchen table, and the two women settled themselves at the other. The cats positioned themselves back to back in the patch of sun on the kitchen floor and were soon fast asleep.

After general conversation and commiseration about the terribleness of the fire and broad questions about future options that were under consideration, Olympia gently guided the conversation back to the table and the reason why Rayna was sitting in her kitchen.

"I'm thinking there's a reason why you came to see me this morning, Rayna, a reason powerful enough that if you'd told me first, it might have kept you from coming at all. Do you want to talk about it?"

Rayna ran her fingers through her hair and nodded. "It's a long story. No, Pastor, it's not a story, it's the truth, and it's also a confession. I started life as a Catholic, and if you are a Catholic, confession is what you do to clean up your act. I'm not a Catholic any more, but I'm still trying to get clean."

"Clean from what?"

Rayna shook her head. "I was going to burn down your church, Pastor, only somebody beat me to it. That really messed me up. But then it woke me up. That's why I came here. I had to talk to you, alone, if you were willing. So thank you."

Olympia kept her voice soft and her words evenly spaced.

"Tell me your truth, Rayna. You can trust me."

"If you don't mind, I'd rather start with the lies. First of all, I don't have cancer. Raggsy is just a dog. He's not a service dog. I've never worked with the elderly, unless you count my taking care of my mother right now. I work part time in a library, and I never owned a car." She took a long swallow of her iced tea, cleared her throat and picked up the tangled narrative.

"My life has been a lie since I left the Catholic Church when I was fifteen. That part is for later. At first it was easy. I made up a past. I invented a person I liked and moved into that body, but then I started losing track of who I told what to. It got harder and harder to stay in the invented person. So I'd change jobs, move or do whatever it took to start over with a new person. And the whole time this is going on, I'm looking to find a way back to God. I kept looking for churches."

"None of them worked for you?"

Rayna shook her head. "They might have, if I'd let them. I never really gave them or myself a chance. I'd come in with all kinds of expectations, and at the first imagined rejection or disappointment I'd hit back."

"You hit back?"

"I started fires. Little fires, not big ones. Trash can or dumpster fires. Fires people would discover before anything really bad happened. Fires to show people that they weren't paying enough attention to what was going on inside their own walls."

"And you never got caught?

She smiled. "Nope. I was smart enough to keep on coming on Sundays for a while after the fire happened. If I suddenly dropped out of sight, they might wonder why, so I always came back for the next couple of weeks and pretended to bet just as shocked and upset as the rest of them were. Then I'd fade away."

"How many times did you do this?"

"Three big ones and several little ones that never made the papers. Some of them got out of hand, did more damage than I expected. I felt bad about that, but in my twisted thinking it was God finishing what I started." She paused. "I told you it was a long story."

"And I'm still listening, Rayna."

"Fast forward and eventually I started coming to South

River. I'd never tried this in a town I'd lived in before, but my mother's getting older, and I don't like leaving her alone all that long. She's starting to have balance issues. She could fall.

"Anyway, I started coming here, as it turns out on your first Sunday. The dog and the cancer thing was always my test. I'd see how people responded, but then something would always go wrong, I'd feel rejected, and I'd want revenge. It almost happened on the first day when the Fosselberg ladies got all bent out of shape because I wanted some water for Raggsy. But they calmed down and even offered me a ride home, and when I said no thanks, they made sure I had water to take with me. I didn't come this Sunday because I was having a change of heart, and I didn't know how to handle it. Then I heard the news about the fire on the TV, and I didn't know what to think. So I called for an Uber and came right over."

She made a sound that might have been a laugh, but sounded more like something caught in her throat. "As you know, I even made cookies for after church on the day of the fire. They're probably still there." She shook her head. "At one point I'm asking myself, is this the next church I'm going to set fire to, and then I'm making cookies. Go figure."

"I think that's why you're here Rayna. I think you are trying to figure it all out." Olympia hesitated, carefully choosing her words. "I think there's still something you're not saying, something that maybe happened when you were fifteen and may be the reason why you left the Catholic Church."

After a long silence Rayna nodded, and she pulled a tissue out of her pocket.

"I think this is going to be one hell of a lot harder than making cookies, Pastor, but its way overdue. I've come this far, so I might as well finish the job."

"What happened when you were fifteen?"

"It happened before I was fifteen. Fifteen was when it stopped because I left. It started happening when I was twelve. I was one of those kids in the Catholic Church everybody read about. I was abused by our parish priest. The thing was, I was a girl. You don't hear too much about the girls that were abused, but believe me, we're out here, and I'm living proof."

Olympia reached for Rayna's hand and held on as she continued with her story. How many hands had she reached for and held in the last two weeks? She was beginning to lose count. Was there no end to it?

"It happens, and you can't tell anyone, because no one would believe you. Shit, you don't believe it yourself. This can't be happening to me, only it is. I suppose the only good thing was that I didn't get pregnant." She held up her hand. "Don't ask."

Olympia continued listening.

"It all fell apart when he found a newer, younger one and pushed me aside. He'd already sworn me to secrecy. Besides, no one would have believed me if I had said anything. But when he moved on, I was devastated. Then I was mad, then I was furious, and then I wanted revenge —revenge on him and eventually anything that was church, and that feeling kept growing, poisoning me inside."

"So you started setting fires."

"No, I started reinventing myself. Like I said, I created a whole new persona, several of them really, and then that person started the fires. The old me, the one who was abused, never would have set a fire, never would have struck back. The old me would have stayed in the confessional and cried her eyes out. The new me set fires and told lies, and then all of that started to collapse when I came to your church. You see, South River was next on the list. I'd even started the scrap book." She pointed to the box at the other end of the table. "I researched the churches and kept records of every fire I set. The big ones got their own books. The little ones were just chapters or short stories. I had it all worked out, only I didn't. Somebody beat me to it. Can you believe that?" She laughed an odd sort of laugh and went on.

"Anyway, like I was saying, after meeting the people there and having them and you be so nice to me, I was starting to have a change of heart. And somebody effing beat me to it. I don't know whether its cosmic irony or divine intervention, but I didn't set this one. Now here I am with my scrapbooks, confessing it all at a kitchen table." She took a breath and bowed her head. "Bless me, Pastor, for I have sinned, and I am heartily sorry for my wrongdoing." She looked up. "Some things you never can forget, can you?"

"That can be a mixed blessing. However, in your case, Rayna, as truly awful as this has been for you, the fact that you do remember it all and you were able to say it out loud to someone who believes you and cares about what happens next is your first step forward. I know people who can help you, and I'll go with you when you're ready."

"You will?"

"I will."

"What about the fires? I set a lot of fires." Again she pointed to the unopened box of scrapbooks.

"First things first, Rayna. One step at a time. I don't think you're going to be setting any more fires."

She shook her head vigorously. "No, Pastor, never again."

"'There is a time to every purpose under the heaven.' I'll help you see it all the way through, I promise. Meanwhile, let's get South River sorted."

"You're including me in that?"

"I am, Rayna."

CHAPTER 46

After speaking with each of the victims individually and getting their permission to go forward with her plan, Olympia introduced Grace Foster, Betty Almasi, Carol Johnson and Ellen Brody to one another on a Skype conference call. At first it was awkward, and the conversation, if you could call it that, was constrained, but eventually they managed to find a date that worked for them all. They would meet Olympia in the late morning of the appointed day at the park-and-drive lot just off the highway in Plymouth. For obvious reasons, Olympia would drive. Some years ago she'd had air conditioning installed in her van, and it seated seven. There would be room to spread out and time to talk and get to know more about one another on the drive.

Olympia called the residence earlier in the day to see if David Cameron was up to receiving visitors. When she was assured that he was, she explained that she would be coming in that afternoon with a couple of the members of his last congregation who wanted to visit him, and they wanted it to be a surprise. She had only one request: Could they please have him in his room so that they could visit privately? And yes, she knew his speech was limited, but his hearing wasn't, and she had visited many people in her work as a chaplain and knew how to communicate by using a tablet or iPad, if necessary.

Thus, as prepared as any of them could be for such a meeting, Olympia included, they climbed into the van. Once inside, they chatted inconsequentially about its interior spaciousness. They asked how long Olympia had owned it but tactfully made no references to age—Olympia's or that of the van. Within moments they were buckled up, literally and metaphorically, good to go.

The drive would be every bit of two hours, more if they hit traffic. Olympia, an excellent driver on the best of days and even better in bad weather, was attuned to their every word, which, after the initial burst of nervous chatter, dwindled to almost nothing. Each woman was alone in a very painful place. Depending on how things turned out, it was hopefully for the last time. Olympia was grateful for the sunshine and the air conditioning. She was grateful for the opportunity to be present to, to be a minister to and a witness to these women as they began their path to healing and wholeness.

When they arrived and parked, Olympia lightened the collective anxiety by thanking the lady who lived inside the GPS for her excellent directions and promising her a second chance at greatness if she could get them all safely home again. Walking closely together, the women entered the building through the glass double doors. Olympia identified them to the receptionist, signed them all in and asked for an escort to take them to visit David Cameron in Room 265.

There were times in her life when Olympia asked for advice and took it. There were other times when she acted completely on her own. Today she was flying solo. She knew if she told Jim or Frederick or even another colleague what she had in mind, they would have done everything to dissuade her, and she wasn't having it. She'd seen those pictures, and having gotten to know some of the women involved, she had witnessed their pain. It all served to strengthen her resolve. She was going way off the radar, and she knew it. There was no training manual for what she was about to do, but there was also little time left in which to do it. The likelihood of anyone dragging a drooling, inarticulate, incontinent, retired minister, who was confined to a wheelchair, before a judge on sexual assault charges was nil. However, no one ever said anything about bringing Lady Justice to confront the old buzzard *in situ*, and Olympia wasn't about to ask permission. These women would finally be able to confront their abuser. They would be in power. They would have the last word. He didn't need further sentencing; he already was in prison.

The volunteer stopped in front of an open door. Olympia could hear the drone of a television talk show.

"David Cameron? Well, here we are, ladies." The white haired, pink smocked escort was as bright and cheery as a coat of fresh paint. "I'll go in first and let him know he has company, then I'll leave you to enjoy yourselves. You know, he's really amazing. Considering the severity of the stroke, he's in great health and sharp as a tack. He could go on for years. Would you like me to have some tea and cookies sent up?"

"I don't think so," said Olympia, "but thank you anyway."

"Okay, then, just remember to sign out at the front desk when you leave, will you?" She lifted a wrinkled, manicured hand and tapped on the door frame before walking in. "David, wakey-wakey, you've got visitors."

The man inside was slumped and dozing in his wheel chair, but hearing voices, he did his best to push himself to a more upright position with his improving good hand. The volunteer, chirping the whole time, stuffed a pillow on his left side, straightened and re-buttoned his sweater and even smoothed his fly-away hair back into place.

"There, now, we're all ready for company. Might even say you look your Sunday best." And then she was gone.

David Cameron was confused and uncomprehending when he looked up at Olympia. It was clear he had no idea who she was, but when the four women who were with her stepped into focus, his initial confusion turned into scarlet-faced rage and shame.

"Hello, David. I'm Olympia Brown, Reverend Olympia Brown. I am serving the church you collapsed in and were carried out of on a stretcher. Yes, that church. The South River Community Church. I've brought some former parishioners of yours who said they wanted to see you."

On the best of days Cameron had difficulty communicating. This was a bad day, and it was only going to get worse. There was no way out, no escape from himself and his actions. He groaned aloud and then dragged the good hand up and covered as much of his face as he could, tears running through his splayed fingers and dripping onto the front of his recently buttoned sweater, his hoarse sobs shaking his now virtually useless body.

Nobody spoke.

Olympia turned to the women and asked the question with her eyes: Do you want to say something to him?

Grace and Carol wordlessly shook their heads but stood their ground and didn't back away. It was Betty Almasi who stepped forward.

"Hello, David. I never thought I wanted to see you again, never thought I could face you after what happened. You broke every shred of faith and trust that I placed in your hands, and when I confronted you that day in the parking lot, you told me about the pictures and what you would do with them if I ever said a word. Well, it worked. I never did, but I never, not for a single day, stopped thinking about the fact that you had them and that you would have power over me for as long as I lived."

The wretched, ragged sobbing continued.

"Rev. Olympia has the pictures, and she was brave enough to reach out to me and the others in love. In love, damn it, love. Not sex, not power, not lust, which commandment would you like, you broke them all, you bastard. Yes, even that one, thou shalt not kill. One of your victims committed suicide. I'll bet you didn't know that, did you? You've scored a perfect ten, and now, you shriveled pile of bones and wasted muscle, you can carry all this to your grave, because I'm not carrying it for one more minute. I'm free. I might not be over it yet, but I'm free of you, and that's a beginning."

Olympia looked at the other two women and again asked with her eyes if they wanted to speak.

Grace Foster stepped forward. "To be honest, I really can't add anything to that. Betty said everything I would have wanted to say, so thank you, Betty." She paused and then continued. "Well, actually, there is something. There's a special place in hell for people like you, David, and I'm sure you'll have plenty of company. It's been a real pleasure seeing you. I understand you could go on for years like this. 'The Lord giveth, and The Lord taketh away.' Isn't that what you told me?"

Carol Johnson, who had remained silent until then, added, "What goes around, comes around, David, and it looks like it just did—all of it, every stinking drop. You've got a lot to think about."

"I found the photographs in the desk," said Olympia. "Right there with the condoms and condom wrappers. I have permission from these women to take the information, not the evidence, to the board. The three women you abused are not going to press charges. We talked about it, and they felt that confronting you was enough. I can't say the same for others who may well come forward once the story gets out." She paused and put her arms around all the women and held them tight. Cameron tried to look away, but his flaccid body would not cooperate.

"One last thing, David. You might be wondering why Ellen is here. She wasn't one of your victims, but she knows what you did, and she's a member of the board. I believe she's what they call a corroborating witness."

Ellen caught Olympia's eye and flicked a quick glance at her watch.

Olympia took a step closer to the helpless man in the chair. "I think it's time we left. By the look of you, it's nap time, or…" she winkled her nose. "Or maybe it's toilet time." Then she softened. "David, you've made a mess of a number of women's lives. You've made a mockery of ministry, and you have abused the trust that so many people invested in you. But you are still alive, and the God I serve is merciful and forgiving to those who confess their sins and truly atone. Of course, that's up to you. Believe it or not, I will pray for you."

The man in the wheel chair jerked his hand away from his face and gurgled,

"F-f-f-f-uck you." And there was not a one of them had any difficulty in understanding him.

CHAPTER 47

The four women walked back out to Olympia's car in stunned silence. Grace was crying, Carol was shaking, and Betty was moving like a robot. Ellen and Olympia, arms outspread, were trying to hold on to them all.

"We need to go somewhere where we can talk this out. There's a nature preserve I know about that's on the way back. They have benches where we can sit. I'll stop and get some drinks at a local coffee shop. How does that sound?"

"I could use something one hell of a lot stronger right now," said Carol, "but coffee's a start."

Minutes later Olympia, turned into the entrance of a woodland wildflower preserve and parked near a tree-shaded seating area. Ellen, seated next to her, was balancing five iced coffees in a cardboard drink holder on her knees.

"I don't know how to explain this," said Grace, "but I feel awful, and I feel great at the same time."

"I had no idea what to expect," said Carol, "and I have to admit that a little piece of me felt sorry for him. But it was a damn little piece, and I know what you mean. I feel like a giant boulder has just been taken off my chest, maybe even pulled out of my heart."

Grace sipped at her coffee. Her time would come.

One by one, each woman in her turn spoke and then listened. Olympia, knowing this was a beginning and not a conclusion said very little until they were getting ready to get back into the car. Then she spoke.

"I want to thank you for your courage and your bravery in coming with me today. We all know healing starts with the first step, and you have all just taken it. Each of your journeys will be different, but you have one another, and you have me, and I strongly suggest you connect with a professionally facilitated survivor group. In fact, I will locate some for you and get you the information. There's so much more, and we'll talk about it on the way back. The one thing you all must hear together is that I will never release your names without your permission, and I will never show anyone the evidence. Your confidence and anonymity is sacred and assured.

"I am, however, going to bring this issue, not your names, to the attention of the governing board of the church. I think they probably know more than they will admit to, but in the true and disgusting nature of this kind of crime, nobody speaks up, nobody believes or defends the victims, and everybody maintains the code of silence. So, my dear friends, I have no idea where this is going to take me. It may well put me out of a job, but I promise you I will not be turning my back on what happened, nor will I be quiet about it."

Before they climbed into the car for the journey home Olympia asked if any of them wanted to press charges or take this further in any way.

Betty seemed to sum it up for everyone. "After today, after having a chance to look him in the eye with all of us standing there, I don't think there's any point. I said what I needed to say. He's as good as dead now, as far as I'm concerned, maybe even more so. Certainly his life as it is now has to be a living hell."

Ellen spoke up. "I'm not one of his victims, but I was one of the silent ones. I had my suspicions, but I never followed up on them. I do, however, agree with Betty that I don't think any good will come from dragging it all through the courts."

"And the papers," added Carol. "I'm damn sure not ready for that."

Ellen continued. "I'll tell you what I am going to do. I am going to make sure everyone in the church knows what happened, no names of course, and that they do something. I have no idea what yet. Make amends, make it right for the women who were victimized and who suffered their humiliation in silence."

"And are still out there suffering." Grace looked down at her hands and chewed on her lip.

Amen to that, thought Olympia. I can only hope I'm around long enough to see how you do it.

CHAPTER 48

Armageddon, the battle to end all battles, the meeting in which the South River Congregation would begin to chart their forward course, was scheduled to take place after the second Sunday service.

Now, after breaking for lunch and no doubt some last minute lobbying, a voting majority of the congregation had regathered in a meeting room provided for their use for as long as they had need of it.

In preparation for this meeting, the final insurance report, the damage assessment from the fire department and restoration company and the projected costs for the various future rebuild/replace/remove entirely options had been delivered and reviewed by the board.

Ted Jennings, now out of the hospital, would have the complete financial records with him with copies available for anyone who wanted one. He flashed Olympia a tight smile as he took his seat at the long table at the front of the room. She wondered what he was thinking. Even though she'd visited him while he was in the hospital, anything of what they talked about was confidential. Ultimately, the final decision of what would happen next, what, or how much he would say today or ever, remained a mystery.

When they were all seated, the latecomers accounted for and the cell phones silenced, Michael Nee thanked them all for coming and called the meeting to order. Olympia raised her hand and was duly recognized.

"If no one objects," she paused, waiting for exactly the effect she wanted to give full weight to the seriousness of the moment, "I wonder if we might begin with a prayer?"

"Please do."

She held up her two hands and asked for guidance in attentive listening, for honesty and compassion in their deliberations and for a vision beyond today in their decision making. Olympia concluded the prayer and walked back to her designated seat at the far right end of the front row—close but not too close, visible but not too visible, a presence, not a power. Nee leaned in toward the microphone positioned on the table in front of him.

"Again, thank you all for coming. I know we've sent electronic and hard copies of the findings and the agenda to the entire congregation so you've all had a chance to go over it, but if there is anyone who needs one, please raise your hand."

Predictably, a few hands went up, and just as predictably, two people asked for something to write with. Olympia stifled her quick flash of annoyance toward those people who come to meetings so thoughtlessly unprepared. Nee tried a second time.

"Ladies and gentlemen, members and friends of South River Community Church, what I am about to say will not be easy for me to say or for you to hear. It is after a number of deep and wrenchingly honest conversations with the board about how, after the devastating fire, we as a congregation should move forward. We come before you with three options. Option one is to tear down the burned sections and restore the building to what it once was. Option two is to tear down and remove the church structure completely and move operations into the newer, relatively undamaged part of the complex and operate out of that until such time as we have a clearer path forward. Option three is to liquidate all assets and completely restructure ourselves and our mission, which may or may not include complete dissolution of the congregation and donating any remaining capital to a worthwhile charity within the town."

The last, complete dissolution, evoked a chorus of gasps and cries and shouts of "no" that temporarily and completely halted the meeting.

Jennings raised his hand. Olympia thought he still looked a little pale, but his voice and posture were confident. She held her breath, wondering but having absolutely no idea what the man was going to say.

When the noise in the room subsided, he said he needed to add a very personal piece of the financial picture, because it would influence the eventual decision. And then he told his story. All of it, concluding with the news that within weeks, after the pending sale of his house, every penny plus interest would be back in the endowment fund. Then he clasped his hands in front of him, bowed his head and begged their forgiveness. After a moment of stunned silence, the people present stood as one body. Some cheered, some cried, and several people pressed forward to embrace him.

Olympia blew out a quiet sigh of relief, and then waited for the next bomb to explode. This would be the worst and most destructive landmine in the history and fabric of the community: the David Cameron bomb. She knew if it was not exposed, defused and thoroughly expunged and eradicated, there could be no real way forward for these people. She watched and waited, having no idea who was going to be brave enough and strong enough to take this on. On the other hand, they could revert to form and never mention it. Then what?

Nee looked quickly to either side of him and recognized Thelma and Selma Fosselberg. Olympia shook her head in disbelief. These were the last two people on earth she ever expected would be the ones to take this on. Both ladies stood, but Thelma was the first to speak. She began by nodding acknowledgment to Ted Jennings.

"That's not all of what we have to think about. This has been quite a month for our little church on the village green." She shook her head, lifted a hand to her lips and took a deep breath. "You may or may not know this, but your governing board has recently been presented with irrefutable, documented evidence of criminal wrongdoing, of repeated instances of sexual misconduct on the part of our previous minister, Pastor David Cameron." She paused again, her voice rising, "It was right under our own roof … and … and we were paying his salary while he was doing it!"

Once again a collective cry of shock and dismay interrupted the speaker. Thelma held up her hand and quieted them down so Selma could continue with her prepared statement.

"It might seem strange for the spinster matriarchs of the church to be the ones to be bring you such unseemly and distressing news, but I assure you, we weren't born yesterday, and one does not spend years in the corporate world without experiencing sexual predators and sexual exploitation. Standing here now, I can say in retrospect that hindsight is 20/20 when you are willing to look. The pattern was clear, but we refused to see it. So we have to admit our own wrongdoing in this. We deliberately looked the other way. We helped to squash the rumors, and we unwittingly, but deliberately, were accessories to these terrible events by allowing them to continue."

Thelma picked up the narrative. "We did know, and we denied it. I don't know how many others of you are sitting here who were part of that conspiracy of silence, but you do. I know that I and my sister and this whole church need to make it right."

Selma picked up the thread, "I believe it is no accident that we are holding our meeting here in this place today. The Jews have a phrase, 'Tikun olam.' It means making it right. It is a core value of Judaism. When things are wrong, you work to make them right. In twelve-step programs, when you have caused harm, you admit it and then you seek to right your wrongs by making amends to those you have hurt or offended. In a couple of weeks, when the time comes for the vote, I'll tell you all right now that I will move that part of our future mission, if we are to have one at all, shall be to right the wrongs committed on our land and in our name."

In the silence that followed the two women sat down and were comforted and embraced by the people on either side of them as Nee stood up. Referring to the agenda, he called them to order once again.

"We have a lot to consider, my friends, but it was never the intention to make a decision at today's meeting. This is a forum. This a place and a time where we can present ideas and points of view and discuss them in the company of all concerned. While I know human nature is not always to speak your truth in front of a group of people, I think, given what we've all just heard, it's about time we started. The floor is open for discussion."

After almost an hour and a half of heated, passionate and sometimes tearful rhetoric, Nee asked for any thoughts or ideas that had not been already expressed. Then he asked for people to put any afterthoughts or insights in writing and mail them to all the members of the board. Finally, he asked, that people not set up a back chain, not hold secret meetings, not form coalitions and not lobby on the side for a particular plan or point of view.

Jeanne Lane raised her hand and was recognized. "You know, when I first heard what you said about Pastor Dave, I was ready to get up and walk out and leave you all to it. I wanted no part of it. But I didn't; I stayed. We can do better, and I, for one, want to stay on now and be part of whatever is going to be."

Olympia, who, other than offering the opening prayer, had remained silent up until then, raised her hand and accepted the microphone. She stood and moved to the front of the room.

"My friends, I am deeply moved by your response and your candor. I have rarely witnessed such bravery and such humility, and I can promise you that if you can continue like this, speaking truth to one another in love and compassion, you will have a future as a congregation. You notice that I do not say a future as a church. A church is not a congregation, it is a building. But a dedicated congregation can make any building, even a garden shed, into a church. Please take all of this home with you and think hard on where you want to go and where you want to be in six months, in a year, and in ten years. That power is yours. You took it back this afternoon. God bless you."

"Thank you, Pastor. While you're up, could you please offer a closing prayer?"

When she finished the prayer and bid them all to "go in peace," nobody moved. They were too shaken by what they'd heard and even more so by what part of it each of them owned.

Finally, one by one, they slowly moved out of the room and into the brilliant July sunshine. Rayna, who had slipped in after the start of the meeting, was now one of the last to leave. She paused only long enough to say, "Thank you, Pastor."

CHAPTER 49

After dinner that evening and after Frederick had been given a line-by-line report on the cataclysmic twists and turns of the day, he said, "Crikey." Then he added, "You can't make this stuff up, can you?" and concluded with, "And now what, good lady wife? Do you think Jim might have some words of advice on this? God knows the Catholic Church has been dealing with this very same thing."

"This one's out of my bailiwick for sure," Olympia said. "I haven't told the board that yet. One crisis at a time, if you don't mind. They will need to call in the big guns, or rather I should say I'm going to recommend they call in the experts. I do know where to find them. I have names and contact information." She paused. "But as bad as it is right now, in the end it's their decision as to how to move forward. I can only offer guidance. They have a long history and culture of looking the other way, of looking inward and covering up rather than opening up."

"I'm thinking about the women," said Frederick. "There are some of them that are still out there. What about them?"

"They're still out there, but many of them have been contacted, and others have been given the opportunity to come forward. I'm working on that along with a couple of the victims independently of the church. In some ways it's a separate issue. It's one that is every bit as important as whether or not to be a church a year from now, but it's still separate. How they treat these women will be part of the entire restoration and reconciliation process. Part of cleaning up the institutional mess, would be another way to put it, and you're right, I do need to talk to Jim."

"God knows the Catholics have been dealing with more than enough of it lately."

"They have been dealing with it for centuries, Frederick, but it's not only the Catholic Church. It's a pretty universal unspoken institutional acceptance and complicity in the abuse of power. When everybody's got a hand in the cookie jar, often for very different reasons —power, money, sex, social position, greed, basically the seven deadly sins—these same people are going to fight like hell to protect, and by any means possible hide, their own vested interests. It's all about CYA—covering your ass."

"So this is church, right? This is what you've dedicated your life to?"

Olympia held up her hand. "No, love, this is some people succumbing to their baser instincts, and we all have them, in the protective shadows of an institution. Government, the entertainment industry, the military, you name it. The church is an institution. I'm still in this business, and despite everything that happened today, I still believe that we do have a higher nature, a better side, a good angel on the other shoulder. I see my job as helping people to find that higher calling and live into it for themselves." She paused for a breath. "And I'm still in the fight."

"In that case, I repeat my earlier question, "What are you going to do?""

"Call Jim, and find out whatever legal issues I need to be aware of in case one of the women needs to know. He can get that for me from his DPD buddy. That's next.

"Meanwhile, as far as the most immediate next steps go? The governing board still has to make the decision either to demolish or restore the church building. What that would involve is one part my next step. The other piece, the abuse and the culture of cover-up, is far more pervasive and in the end will be the making or the breaking of the community. So they have to look at what they are really going to tear down before they can choose if and how and what they will rebuild. This is meaning of life stuff here."

"What about the embezzled money?"

"Actually, that's the easiest one of all. Ted has a property worth far more than what he, uh, borrowed. He can recoup all the money through the sale of that property and return every penny with interest, which is what he is doing. Since he's a widower without children, there's no one to contest it." She shook her head. "He's a good man who made a poor choice and then got caught up in shame and denial, then more lies to keep it hidden. To be honest, when I think about it, he may have done them all a favor by starting that fire."

Frederick cocked a questioning eyebrow in her direction.

"He forced the issue, both issues really. Now they have no choice but to dig deep inside themselves in order to move forward. It means looking hard at some things that are really pretty ugly. But if church is about forgiveness and restoration and cleaning up your spiritual act, so to speak," she paused and chewed on her lip, "they will or they won't, but at least they've got the opportunity."

"So what about Cameron?"

She made a face. "'Judge not lest ye be judged,' is one way of looking at it, and so is the idea of just desserts. Let's just say the man made his bed, and now he's sleeping in it and wearing diapers to boot. How the mighty have fallen. He's just mad he got caught. The man is not the issue. He's a symbol of what went wrong, not the cause. How the church will handle it, like the road not taken, will make all the difference." She held up her finger. "And that, my love, is what remains to be seen. Will they, or won't they?"

She looked at her watch. "Yikes, I'd better call Jim."

August 1667

I think my beloved Aunt Louisa would be very proud of me. In truth, it may well have been her mischievous spirit which suggested a way to confront the gossip and put an end to it once and for all.

I learned through some discreet questioning here and there that the spinster Bradford twins, Mary and Martha (They always were a couple of dried-up old biddies.) are the ones who have been making the unkind assertions with regard to my friendship with Susan, assumptions and dark innuendoes which they feel compelled to speak of to anyone they meet.

So, knowing how shamelessly nosey they are, Susan and I decided to invite them to tea on a Sunday afternoon so they could have a good look for themselves. There, in the privacy of our living room, we four made light conversation. The sisters were looking around the room like two matching owls, their heads turning in all directions. It was all Susan and I could do to keep from laughing aloud.

We played it all out as though we had been rehearsing for weeks. We made a great show of tending to each other's preferences and smiling fondly at one another. The twins, with their owl-eyes getting bigger and bigger, were beginning to lose their words in evident dismay when the clock on the mantle struck four.

That was the signal for Susan's husband, Charles, still weak from his war injuries, my 'husband' Richard, Lottie, the freed slave who has joined our family and her daughter, Emmalee, my son Jonathan and Susan's daughter, Clarinda—even Sammy the cat, to tumble into the room. We watched as the four owl-eyes started blinking faster and faster. I confess I was forced to leave the room to giggle in private. All of us now, our patchwork family of men, women and children, continued the ridiculous farce with light and engaging conversation about our lives and families. Then, slowly we directed the conversation to the school that Susan and I, and eventually Lottie, when her reading skills are improved, were about to open. We said, without so much as crossing our fingers behind our backs, that being the women of substance and influence they clearly were, we hoped the Misses Bradford would honor us with their presence on our opening day. How could they not agree?

More anon, LFW

CHAPTER 50

While not exactly a reveal party in the customary sense, the early September evening with Jim and Andrew was meant to be revelatory. It was intended to be a first viewing of Frederick's finished water garden, complete with color-changing fairy lights that turned on with a click of the wand, natural rock waterfall and celebratory dinner party. Of course, all of that had to wait until it was suitably dark to be properly appreciated. Thus, the pre-dinner drinks and tiny tid-bits part of the evening was going on far longer than anticipated. But nothing is without its benefits, and the extended time gave Olympia ample opportunity to provide Jim and Andrew with the final chapter of the religious drama she'd been living through for most of the summer.

"So when do you start back to the church? Must be pretty soon."

"I'm not going back, Jim, at least not to South River.

It took me a while to convince them that I wasn't the right person for the job, and I'm not. They need a so-called after pastor, a person especially trained to help a congregation after a misconducting minister. Talk about a special calling, but I'm not it."

"What was the final outcome then?" Jim was carefully arranging his snacks in a semicircle on his paper plate.

"Well, as you can imagine, they had meetings all summer long, but they finally got themselves to the point where they could vote."

"Come on, girlfriend, don't keep a man hanging."

"Pretty amazing really. They voted to repair and restore the rear part of the building that wasn't badly damaged and create a chapel or worship space in that area. The badly damaged part, the church itself, has been completely razed, gone. At some point in the not too distant future, after the first reconstruction is done, they are going to put up a multi-use building on the site and offer the use of it to the town."

"What exactly is that?" asked Andrew.

"As I understand it, it will be a kind of community activity center, a place for AA meetings, community service activities, even a stage for local performers and coffee house presentations. The plans are still in progress, but it's a wonderful idea."

"Okay, that's the building taken care of, but what about the sexual misconduct thing? What did they do about that?"

"In a word, after much wailing and gnashing of teeth, they owned it, and after a few more meetings, they agreed to hire an after pastor, a trained professional for this kind of situation, to help them rebuild themselves from the ground up."

"That took courage."

Olympia blew out a long breath. "Tell me about it. I don't mind saying there was more than one occasion this summer when I was ready to just turn tail and run, but since I'd started it, I felt compelled to see it through before I handed it on."

"What about the women you contacted?'

"Well, already I told you about their visit to Cameron. After that no one really wanted to take it any further as far as the man himself, but they all did go for professional help. Two of them, one of the survivors and an advocate from the church, went on to start a survivors' support group. Who knows, maybe it will keep going, and one day they will be able to hold their meetings in the new community center, but I'm getting ahead of myself. I won't have any say in the matter, and that's the way it should be."

"It's been quite a journey for you, hasn't it, Olympia?"

"Not by half, Jim, but we made it through to the other side, and I think we are all better for it. I'm ready for a vacation or at least a break. I'm not looking for anything for a while."

"If I believe that, good lady wife, I might as well buy the bridge you're selling. And I don't know about you, but I'm getting hungry. If I have another glass of wine, I will fall asleep, and we wouldn't want that, now, would we?"

"Everything's in the oven, ready to go."

"I never asked what we're having." Jim unseated one of the cats and got up out of his chair.

"An old stand-by: mushroom and spinach lasagna, garlic bread and Caesar salad. You can load up your plates in the kitchen, grab a tray and come on back out here so we can enjoy the sunset."

"No china, no polished silver, no white damask table cloth?"

"Maid's day off," retorted Olympia. "We're just gonna have to rough it."

WHEN THE SUN WAS FULLY DOWN, THE MEAL WAS finished and the garden outside the conservatory was in darkness, Frederick switched to preparation mode. Because he was English, he never would never admit that he was just the teensiest bit nervous about the outcome of this whole thing. "Keep calm and duck the flying shrapnel," was his working motto, but the moment of truth was upon him. Jim and Andrew and Olympia had all turned their chairs to face outward so as best to observe the main event.

"Lights," said Frederick. He flipped a switch, and a pleasing arrangement of low level lights came on, illuminating the pond.

"What's that in the pond?' asked Olympia. "I can see something moving."

"I have installed a mating pair of koi for you. Their names are Romeo and Juliet. They know their names, and they come to call. I snuck them in while you were putting together the lasagna."

"Wonderful," said Olympia.

"And now the waterfall." Frederick went outside and pulled down a lever that released the water in the rain-water holding tanks that would gravity-feed the falls. After waiting a moment or two to ascertain that the water was indeed moving, and moving in the right direction, he returned. Back in the conservatory he held up a remote control wand, aimed it at the pond, clicked it and called out, "More water, more lights."

Olympia was holding her breath. This was Frederick. Things happened when Frederick got creative.

"Ta-dahhh!"

In that moment the water began to flow down over the rocks, multi-colored garden-fairy lights twinkled from behind the tumbling water, the fish swam in happy concentric circles—and nothing else happened. The damned thing worked. No unplanned independent geysers, no flaming short circuits, no fried fish. It worked and worked beautifully.

"There now," said Frederick, "your very own fish pond and waterfall."

"Frederick?"

"Mmmm?"

"It's beautiful."

September 1867

The summer is drawing to a close, and Susan and I will soon be opening the doors of our school to the first ten students. I must note that the Misses Bradford have, since the day of the tea party, remained curiously silent on the subject of my friendship with Susan. But in recalling that day I am reminded of something my grandmother from Yorkshire used to say when she became vexed with someone and didn't understand their actions.

"There's now't so queer as folk, 'cept thee and me." Then, shaking her finger in my face, she'd add, "...and times I even wonder after thee."

More Anon, LFW

EPILOGUE

The headline read, 'South River Community Church Reopens Its Doors.'

After two years in the remaking, like Phoenix rising out of the ashes, members of the South River Community Church have announced they are once again open for business and all are invited to join them in the celebration.

"It's a miracle really," longtime member and church moderator, Selma Fosselberg, is quoted as saying. "We thought we'd lost everything. Then we learned we hadn't lost everything we valued at all, we'd just lost sight of it. Now we have made it our mission to be a true community church with a genuine community mission and vision. Our doors are now open to all."

"And not just on Sundays," added her twin sister, Thelma Fosselberg. "We plan to make our newly constructed community space available for the use of those who have need of it."

On Sunday evening, September 21, the public is warmly invited to the service of renewal and rededication and to meet the newly installed minister, Pastor Dorothy Hughes. This will be followed by a champagne, tea and just desserts reception.

THANK YOU SO MUCH FOR READING! IF YOU'D LIKE TO be notified when the next book releases, please join my email list. I generally release twice a year. Read on for a sneak peek...

SNEAK PEEK

Want more Olympia?

Want to start at the beginning?

Here is an excerpt from the **very first in the Olympia Brown Mission Mysteries.**

A Twisted Mission

Without warning the snake slashed and zigzagged across the path just inches from his feet. He almost stepped on it. With his heart racing and sweat breaking out everywhere, he watched as the moving grasses off to his right indicated the direction of the reptile's speedy escape.

He straightened up and looked around to see if anyone had witnessed the incident but saw no one. He was morbidly afraid of snakes and had been since the day his father, drunk and trying to make a man of him, threw one in his face and then laughed when he screamed, fell on the ground and wet himself. The only thing he feared more than snakes these days was someone finding out about it. This was a close call, but so far his luck was holding. No one saw it. His shameful secret was still safe. When his breathing and heart rate returned to normal, he continued walking along the sandy path toward the crew shack. To be on the safe side, he stamped his feet, flapped his arms and made as much noise and commotion as he could.

Across the street and up the short hill from the camp ground, a painfully thin and desperately unhappy young man scribbled a few words on a scrap of paper, folded it in half and pushed it deep into his jeans pocket. Then he climbed up on top of the battered old wooden dresser next to his bed. Careful to keep his balance, he tossed one end of a twisted sheet up and over the ceiling beam directly above him. He knotted it, yanked on it to test its strength and then secured it. Once that was done, he tied the other end around his neck. He had taken great care with the measurements so that when jumped off and kicked the shoddy dresser away from beneath him, his feet would not reach the floor. He hoped, even dared to pray, it would be quick.

A fiftieth birthday, whatever else it might be, is a milestone. It can be a warning signal, a turning point or both. It can be loudly celebrated or quietly ignored, but it cannot be denied. It is a time when many will choose to step back and take stock. The Rev. Dr. Olympia Brown had just reached that significant event with as many questions in her mind as she had years logged onto the calendar. The two at the very top of the list were, should she continue as a college chaplain and professor of humanities and religion at Merriwether College, or should she change direction, leave academia and take on a full time parish ministry?

On the nonprofessional and more personal front there were more questions. Now that her two sons, Malcolm and Randall, were technically out of the safe suburban nest, her status as a not-very-swinging single was lonely. Maybe she should be more proactive about creating a little more action in that corner of her life. Maybe she should move out of her white, middle class, three-bedroom expanded cape in the town with the good schools that she needed when the boys were young and buy a condo in Boston or Cambridge. That would certainly ease her commute and save money on gas.

She could take her mother's advice, let nature take its course and wait for the universe to reveal what the future might offer—but Olympia rarely took her mother's advice, so she eliminated that one even before she wrote it down. And so it was on a spectacular summer day in early June, she was sitting in her back yard, sipping iced tea and making a list … or maybe it was a five-year plan —she hadn't decided which. In big block letters she created three columns across the top of the sheet of paper: Done, Yet to be done, and Wishful thinking bucket list.

If nothing else, and there was a whole lot of else, Olympia Brown was methodical and well organized. She typically set reasonable goals for herself and then in her own determined fashion strategized how to reach them. At age fifty, she knew who she was and pretty much what she wanted out of life. She also knew what she was and was not prepared give up in order to bring that about, or so she thought.

However, nothing that was about to happen in the coming summer was on this list and no one, not even Olympia, the practical plotter, could have predicted or planned for what did happen. She couldn't possibly know it, but it seemed she was at the mercy of a host of gods and goddesses who were bored and decided to have a bit of fun. The object of their ungodly mischief of fancy and foolishness was a middle-aged, slightly restless college professor who in one unguarded moment said she might be ready for a change. She looked again at the sheet of paper in her lap, made a face, and scrawled, "None of the above." Then she crumpled the paper and tossed back and high over her shoulder.

She decided to take a second look at the invitation she'd received to be a summer chaplain at Orchards Cove in Maine. A summer of fresh sea air and camping under towering pines in a seaside village would be a refreshing change and give her plenty of time to think about her future. Would it not?

Olympia's mother also told her, "Be careful what you wish for." It would have been good advice, had she listened, but she didn't, and therein hangs the tale.

To read the Olympia Brown Mysteries in ebook, print or audio, click here.

They are also available in libraries, and if all else fails, contact the author at:

www.juithcampbell-holymysteries.com

ABOUT THE AUTHOR

Rev. Dr. Judith Campbell is a community-based Unitarian Universalist minister. She has authored twelve books in the popular Olympia Brown Mystery series and has started a second series, The Viridienne Greene Mysteries.

She has published poetry, children's books, two books on watercolor painting, and several articles on religion, spirituality, and the arts. She lives by the sea in Plymouth, Massachusetts, with her husband, Chris Stokes, along with their two cats.

Writing is her passion, her challenge, and the most authentic way she can live into her life and her ministry. What she attempts to do with her writing is to raise awareness around current social and ethical issues that affect us all... and therein hangs a tale... a very good tale.

Judith is available in person or on Skype to speak to your book group or at your library. As a minister and teacher, she is available to lead workshops and retreats on fiction, memoir, and spiritual biography. Please contact her and get on her mailing list through her website, www.

judithcampbell-holymysteries.com, or through her two Facebook pages: Judith Campbell, and Judith Campbell Author. She loves to hear from her readers and responds personally to every email.

Made in the USA
Middletown, DE
15 July 2020